All You Need Is A Hug

All You Need Is A Hug

The wonders of love

Kriss Venugopal

PARTRIDGE

ISBN: Hardcover   978-1-5437-0260-6
               Softcover   978-1-5437-0259-0
               eBook   978-1-5437-0258-3

To order additional copies of this book, contact
Partridge India
000 800 10062 62
orders.india@partridgepublishing.com

www.partridgepublishing.com/india

Contents

My Gratitude is to God …
Dedicated to my life …
Thanks for teaching me to live,
Thanks for what I've got. I give
Thanks for the paths shown,
Thanks for the known and unknown,
Thanks for the moments I cherish,
Thanks for the fears and anguish,
Thanks for the moments that brought tears,
Thanks for those that brought cheers.

A note about the hug

A forethought. I need to tell you about a hug. A hug is a medicine, it's a gift of love, it's a way to express that you care, it's how you share the warmth in your heart, it's a language between those who share the hug and it is the affirmation of what we agree upon. It is a way to celebrate a special moment, it is what tells you what you have in your heart and cannot put in words. It is much more than that can be ever expressed in words.

Like in a Bollywood film, it is simply the magical *Jadu ki Jhappi*. It cures all ills and makes way for the better. I was told once that

"All you need is a hug"

And yes, when you have memories that keep haunting you, all you need is a hug. Hug the memories and make the best out of it too.

This book has many characters whom you would have met in your life and some whom you know so well or it could be you too. It is not about the central character or the characters around him. This book is a collection of memories that keep hugging us. It is a collection of the precious moments that keep coming back to us. So the next time if someone gifts you a precious moment, the apt and rightful expression of gratitude is nothing but a hug.

1

The journey begins

"Sir... sir..."

Benson called Kannan from behind the wheels while maneuvering the vehicle to the side, which woke Kannan up from the slumber, which he had slid into in the back seat of the car, hugging a soft pillow like a kid. The hybrid engine made no sounds and the silence was broken by the sweet melodious songs being played on the CD player. It was Kannan's personal collection of his favourite old songs. Each one reminded him of something or someone. Many of us, like Kannan, would have songs that kindle thoughts and some songs take us back in time. This was how Kannan took the long trips with Benson, his trusted charioteer, *sarathy* as Kannan would refer him to. Kannan wiped his face on the soft hand towel he had. He turned to Benson rubbing his eyes.

"Have we reached?" asked Kannan eagerly.

"No sir. A few minutes more. And sir, you have a call," Benson smiled with the phone in his hand stretched towards Kannan.

He took the mobile from Benson, who had kept it on charge. He carefully wore his spectacles. As Benson got back on the road and drove smoothly through the road at a steady pace and the morning road seemed to welcome them to glide away without much traffic. Kannan checked the phone and the messages while checking the roads outside from time to time. His smile said it all. Keeping the phone aside Kannan eased on to the comfort of the soft leather seats with his hands behind the back of his head. The trip was dear to his heart; a journey back in time. A journey through the narrow lanes of life he walked. The roller coaster ride through the troughs and crests he had travelled through all the seven special decades.

Within a few minutes the car slowly came to a halt near a gate. The gate which was never closed until late night till the wee hours of the morning. The sun never saw it closed for sure. It had all the houses of Appa's brothers, and the two dear houses in which Kannan spent his childhood. The morning sun was up and the slanting rays had just started warming up the rain washed roads and trees. Kannan got out of the car and stood there before the gate. He took a deep breath and smiled with eyes closed, as if he wanted to hold the happiness within his eyes, not letting out even a single memory. But a small tear drop found its way through the wedge of the eyelids. Those eyes had seen many slide down through the life - happy and sad ones. That's what makes it so special. Some wipe away the pain leaving a fresh picture in the mind forever and some add a wet pain forever in the heart. But this one tear was a special one; the one which found its way from a heart overflowing with happiness.

The phone rang again, and Kannan cut the call. He wanted no one to take away the pleasure of that very moment. Kannan went towards the closed gate and touched the wet, rusting gate. The cold touch on the metal gate moist with rainwater ran shivers down Kannan's spine. It was not fear, it was not happiness, it was neither sadness nor pain.

It was as if little Kannan was jumping out of the old man's body and running to the homes. Little Kannan, who ran from one door to another in the gated compound, which had the homes of his uncles and aunts and for very long, Kannan did not know that they were different houses. It was his home. His age was just a number as the kid in him was wanting so much to run towards the doors and rush to the dear and near ones. But as they say with old age comes wisdom, Kannan realized that they were not the same homes where the warmth made everyone smile, where the love made every morsel of food tastier and every day was a celebration. Kannan kept looking at the houses, silently. He did not know whether it was just few minutes or hours that he stood there. But it all felt like a few seconds, flashing through all those stories behind that very gate which remain closed today.

Kannan held the hand of the little boy who was running out from his heart. Held his hand tightly and pulled him back. Kannan told the kid in his heart something every parent would have to their kids.

"Come come... there are so many other places to go and see... so much to enjoy... this is just one of them."

Kannan smiled and walked back to the car. Got himself comfortable on the front seat pushing it back to his convenience. He kept the happy grin on his face intact and told Benson, clicking the seat belt to a lock as if it were a race.

"So where to next as per plan?"

Benson checked the list of places Kannan had meticulously written in the book he had handed over to him, checked and said, "Sir it's your school."

The list was long, a journey filled with thrills. But it had just begun. Deep inside his heart, Kannan could feel the happy kid in him enjoy the moments as he is the one who travelled all this while. Kannan took the shades from the glove compartment of the car and wore it with a smile.

"Chalo," said Kannan.

Race it was; a race of memories back in time. As the car moved forward, Kannan took the phone and wrote out a message.

"Safe and sound... back in time... will keep you posted" and clicked the send button.

2

Half an hour

As usual, the lights went off. It was the scheduled power cut in the city, which plunged the street in darkness. His old hands searched for the match box. Carefully with the shaky hands he lit a match and lit a candle. His eyes were wet with tears, face frilled with the eighty years of his life, most of which went in the toil for his two children. He lifted the candle and moved towards the hall. The walls had pictures of his children, their spouses and a few with their mother. He lit another candle on one corner of the room. The room lit up in the candlelight like the early morning skies. He could hear the buzz outside on the streets. He thought to himself, "If ... If I could spend some time with my children, I would have been in those pictures."

With a big sigh and trembling hands, he picked his spectacles and the letter beneath it. It was the print out of an email his son had sent him from abroad.

> *Dear Appa*
>
> *I would be coming home on the 25th. I will manage the transportation from the airport. Don't bring the car please. You need to take rest. I had called Amma. She is coming on the 1st. She is fine with Akka. Hope you are doing fine. Do you need anything from Dubai?*
>
> *Your son*

He would have read the letter over a hundred times but kept reading it. He had a whole lot of emails, which had the typical corporate language his son was used to, printed and filed in his office table. This one was the latest. Waiting for his son was not easy as age had made him frailbut kept the smile when tears of joy rolled down the ridges of his cheeks from the corner of his eyes. The eyes, which never got time to look at his son grow as all that while he was working to provide the best he could for his children.

He looked at the ticking clock and was eagerly waiting for his son to arrive. He never knew to express his love with hugs or words. He only had the smiles and nothing but that. He went and checked the phone in the darkness twice, checking whether there was a call. He looked at the mobile his son had given him the previous year again and again. No calls yet.

Went to the door and opened it to check whether his son has reached. No one yet at the door. He would again and again look out of the window to see a cab coming or rush to the door when he hears a car stopping by. Slowly time passed and he was very impatient to see his son. Every moment of his life was filled with the urge to show the love for his sonbut was worried whether he would be spoilt with the amount of love he had for him. He thought to himself, "It's been so long. He is grown up now. He has his family. Will he feel strange if I hug him?"

He heard the bell ring while he was lost in thought. He got up from the chair and he opened the door with a smile, "Ah. How was the flight? Did you have something?"

He stopped at that with his heart beating so fast in excitement and the desire to hug his son with all the warmth in his heart.

"It was ok ... slept well. The fringe benefit of flying business class."

He said, while he hid the desire to hold his Appa tight to himself in a hug. But held himself backthinking, what he might think.

"If you have had dinner, have fruits. Shall I make a coffee for you?"

He asked trying to express his affection still looking at him as he used to look when he camehome from the office.

"Take rest. What plans for tomorrow? Do you have any meetings scheduled?"

He said in his firm voice, which hid the love in his heart. And prayed in his heart that he says that he would spend the day with him, the whole day, just to be with him and nothing but that.

"Yes. I have a morning meeting with clients and a few other lined up for the day," said the son. His heart sank and tried not to show it to his beloved son, as he never wanted to be a stumbling block in anyone's life, least to his own son.

"I have made your bed in the ac room, it is nice ... I will sleep in the other room" Appa said.

"Bzzzzzzzz... Bzzzzzzzzz…"

The usual smart phone buzz echoed the room, when his son picked up the call and started talking.

"Hello. Yeah... reached safe... ok ... ok."

He looked at his father's eyes wet with tears. He was looking tired and seemed sad. He paused for moment and continued with his call.

"I can be there by 9 at best... ok ... ok."

He saw his Appa making coffee for him.

"Appa still knows my likes and dislikes. He knows I want coffee," he thought to himself.

"I have these few days and I will be back with my work and ..."

Appa was bringing the small mug full of coffee sweet with his love for his son. Seeing his son on the phone he kept the mug on the table and pointed at it, asking him to have it while it is hot. Still on the phone busy scheduling meetings the son saw his Appa walk slowly in the cold darkness of the night towards his room inside, where he would spend time watching TV and sleep off in the chair.

"Can you do me a favor? Can you postpone the meetings and schedule the same after two days? Ok, thanks a ton," he said quickly.

The phone went silent as he cut the call. He stood up and walked towards his Appa.

"Appa," he called, "Can I spend a day only with you, not doing anything else?"

The room was filled with the candle light, silence and the love alone. The father and son looked at each other for a moment. Four eyes had a few drops of love in them. And for the first time, without thinking anything they hugged each other. That was the best warm, loved and blessed half an hour of both their lives. The lights came on, after the load shedding exercise of the electricity board. Or was it love that brought the brightness to their lives.

3

Kannan breaks a record

Days in Bangalore are always fun. The walk through the brigade street or a visit to the cafes on the sidewalks, the cool breeze, the smell of roast corn on the cob, the street vendors selling cheap jewelry, fashion accessories, belts, jackets, purses and a lot more. Kannan loved Bangalore as there is a part of his infanthood associated to the city, which was much greener then. Since the time he remembered Bangalore winds had a special smell. The aroma of fun and frolic. Laid back attitude of people who would live enjoying their lives with a smile on their faces irrespective of the strata of the society they belonged to. The streets would satisfy the low, the sidewalks for the middle and the cafes, pubs and restaurants for the high class. There was something for everyone.

Though he does not remember much, the Kannada he heard from his mother, a few vacations and his personal visits had made the city close to his heart. The banners and hoardings on both sides of the road, the shops, the cars, and the people who loved living their life enjoying it were all sights worth a look more for Kannan. Bangalore was more of the Rio of India if Mumbai (I would prefer to say Bombay) was the New York and Delhi was the London. Every evening most of the streets would have the fervor of a carnival.

Kannan's eyes were stuck on the first look on the sidewalk where he saw a man dressed in the usual vendor style with his khaki pants, blue sweater and a strange brown monkey cap. The evening breeze was cool and he was trying to bear the cold and hang a few LP discs, the name popularized by the long play vinyl discs, on the wall on to the hooks he had arranged on ropes. Old LP records for gramophone and record players. The age of the LP discs and the juke boxes are gone and the prospective clients the man was looking for were the ones who vouch the quality and the grains of the vinyl discs or those who would like to have a part of the history on their walls as antiques. Kannan walked towards the guy.

"Namaskara sir.Enu bekku?" he asked what Kannan wanted in Kannada.

By instinct the reply came out, "Idera LP disc bele eshtu?" with his eyes shining excitement.

"Aivaththu rupya," was his reply.

50 rupees per disc! Kannan was excited at the best bargain he could ever get. He started searching through the whole bundles of discs. Old ones, classics, devotional - the collection was so huge, Kannan knew that if he let his mind into buying, it would cost him a fortune as all of them were so luring.

He saw a disc - a 45 rpm short play disc with red label in the middle. The black shellac disc had the name *Sholay* written on it. He remembered the songs so well. He had the disc and started smiling to himself.

It was a regular event at home when Venki Mama used to come for vacations to dance to the tunes of the songs played on the record player. Appa always played MS Subbalakshmi classical and devotional songs, but Venki mama and the four year old Kannan always chose film songs and the few English discs of Usha Iyer, who later became popular as Usha Uthup. The black Odeon Discs knew the time when they would be picked up by Venki mama and carefully placed on the turning disc on the record player. Then he would catch hold of the needle arm by its ears and place it on the shining black groove after switching the rpm knob and start the player. The needle when it rests on the groove, starts moving towards the inner circles of the record and the song would be heard after the initial hiss of the player. Then it was dance time for Kannan and Venki Mama.

It was another vacation for Venki Mama and the usual dance sessions where on when Amma was returning from her tailoring classes.

"Venki, here is a disc of *Sholay*. I borrowed it from my teacher," said Amma.

The name of the teacher sent shivers down the spine of Kannan. He was scared of the tailoring teacher who used to comehome for tea sometimes. It was a big black mole on her face that scared Kannan.

"Great. Kanna, time for a new dance," said Venki Mama to Kannan.

He played the record and Kannan heard the Hindi song which even remains close to his heart till date.

O0000 ....mehbooba ... O.. mehbooba ....

They danced to the song over and over again till they dropped exhausted laughing. For the next two weeks the record found its top position at home for Venki and Kannan.

That morning it was time for Venki to leave and bags were packed. Kannan stood there by the door with a sad drooping face that his playmate was leaving. He had tears in his eyes, when Venki came and hugged him tight.

"Don't worry. I will be back soon," said Venki to Kannan which brought a smile back to his face.

Venki Mama left and Amma had her tailoring classes.

"Kanna... be a good boy. I will be back soon. If you want anything ask Periyamma. Okay?" said Amma waving to him with her black two fold umbrella and her brown floral pattern saree and black oval bakelite spectacles.

As Amma walked out of sight, Kannan ran to the cupboard where the records were kept. He pulled the *Sholay*disc to play and it slipped from his hand. Kannan's heart started pounding seeing the edge of the disc break and a piece fall apart. The face of the tailoring teacher came to his mind. Her anger was so evident in Kannan's thought, when she would come to know that her disc was broken. For the next hour, Kannan could not do anything. He kept running from room to room trying to find a place to hide. His heart was still beating fast.

"Oh what have I done? Amma will scold me. No, she will be furious.No, she will beat me. What will Appa say? What will the teacher say?" thoughts ran wild in Kannan's mind.

The next sight doubled his fears. He saw Amma walking towards home with the tailoring teacher.

"Why did she have to come today itself? Oh, she is coming to take her record back. Now what to do?" Kannan started sweating. His throat went dry, heart beats were more like drum beats at its crescendo.

Amma and her teacher walked into the home to find no one around and the door was open.

"Kanna ...." called Amma.

Kannan could hear the muffled calls but did not respond. Amma kept calling finding no response.

"Maybe he has gone to his Periyappa's house," Kannan heard Amma telling the teacher

Amma seated the teacher in the hall and walked into the room to keep her bag.

"Teacher I stitched the frock, you taught me.... please come inside... I want to show you"

Kannan heard the footsteps and the heart was in a roll. Amma opened the cupboard to take the frock out and she screamed.

She saw Kannan crouched among the clothes on the second shelf inside the cupboard with the broken record clenched in his hands. Amma and teacher had a laugh when they realized what had happened. The 'record-breaking' attempt was successful and since then the memories of the dance and music also had a companion - the 'record-breaking' attempt.

Kannan thought about his antics in the childhood while he decided the LP discs he would buy. The man in his monkey cap counted the discs and took money from Kannan. He walked with the white plastic bag with the LP records with a smile on his lips. He brushed his long hair with his fingers back which flew in the breeze and kept smiling. The cover had the record which brought back the sweet memories on the top and it read.

Sholay

4

Dining out

"Good evening, sir," greeted the restaurant manager in crisp grey suit and white shirt. A well-trimmed beard and a smile fixed on to his lips. Five-star hospitality at its best, thought Kannan seeing him. Kannan smiled back with a grace which was so much a part of his lifestyle.

"Do you have a reservation?" he asked.

"Yes, I stay in Room 411," replied Kannan.

"Oh is it? Pleasure to welcome you sir and you are our privileged customer. Please come this way," said the suave manager and led Kannan to the table.

Kannan was in his relaxed favorite attire, a long brush cotton beige colored kurta and pure white pyjamas.

The manager pulled the chair and smiled to offer the seat to Kannan. Waved out to the service waiter to attend to the special guest. The slim young gentleman in black and black came towards Kannan and greeted him.

"Good evening sir. My name is Vaibhav and I would be happy to take care of your needs this evening," said the smiling young man.

"Get me something light and special," said Kannan.

"Sure sir. I will take the privilege to place the order on your behalf," said Vaibhav and moved towards the Open kitchen counter in the huge restaurant. He returned in a while with an exotic tropical refresher as the welcome drink.

"Sir, this is our special welcome drink for you with fresh orange juice, sliced banana, diced mangoes, watermelonand pineapple over crushed ice. Enjoy," said Vaibhav.

Sipping the welcome drink, Kannan was reminded of the weekly outings he had with his family. He was reminded of Appa who never bothered to get himself new clothes but would clothe Kannan and Pachai with the best possible. He was reminded of Amma who would be ready to give them all the food, even if it means to go hungry herself. He was reminded of the happy moments they shared, the trips, the Sunday morning breakfast which Appa used to bring home, the evening outings and the film and a treat at the restaurant.

Sunday was the day when Appa would pick a movie to watch, and post the film, would be a dinner at a restaurant. Nothing high flying but a fun outing for a normal middle class family. During one such outing, after watching the film 15 year old Kannan walked out looking at others, with airs around him like the hero of the film. Appa, Amma and Akka joined him in a while. They got into the car and everyone knew the destination Arul Jyothi.

Car was parked, and they entered the restaurant, where the manager in white and white smiled seeing the regular weekly customers. His smile was so broad and bright like a tube light in its full power. The hotel had glass showcases with different varieties of sweets and savories. The smell of dosa and chutney filled the air with the smell of burning agarbathies in front of the Gods' pictures. As they walked in Kannan saw the glass refrigerator with soft drinks with the glass frosted with the moisture. They walked in and sat down to order. The smiling waiter raised his eye brows at Kannan as it was his way of greeting him.

"Sir, soup?" asked the waiter.

"No. What do you have?" asked Appa.

He listed out the dishes in his nonstop regular style.

"Dosa, nei roast, rocket masal, masal dosa, idly, borotta, uthappam, chapaththi, poori, chola puri, koththu porotta, upma, pongal ..."

Hardly could Kannan understand the rest, but heard his favorite chola puri in between and quickly retorted out in excitement.

"I want chola puri.

Appa smiled and placed the order asking Amma and Akka too.

"Nei roast," said Akka.

"Poori," said Amma.

"One plate chapatti kurma, one nai roast, one set poori and one chola puri," said Appa.

Then it was the waiting time when the discussion was on about the film they had just watched, with topics from inside the family about someone getting married, some function to be attended, someone coming in search of a job and so on till the food arrived. Then it would be silence except for the munching sounds around the table. The aroma of the fresh coconut chutney, the masala, the chole, the sliced onions, the raita, the crisp dosa roasted to perfection like paper in ghee, and the aroma of the fluffy poori in full bloom like balloons.

The eating ends with the waiter coming to take the dessert order.

"Sir, kafi, tea, juice, rose milk?"

"One masala milk for me," said Appa.

"I want rose milk," said Kannan.

Akka smiled and said "Me too."

Amma was silent.

Appa asked her "Don't you want anything?"

Amma shrugged her shoulder and gestured that she did not want anything.

Akka, Kannan and Appa finished the last course and waited for the bill. Amma went on talking about Venki Mama, Swami Mama and about a few others which was not much of interest to Kannan. He walked to the sweet show case and stood there looking at them. Appa paid the bill and walked out and tapped Kannan's shoulder and kept the hand on his back as they walked towards the car. As they slowly drove through the slowly sleeping town roads and reached home Kannan noticed Amma's face. The car stopped in front of the house and Appa parked the car. As they walked out Kannan noticed again at Amma's face a strange silent expression.

"Amma, why are you silent? What happened? Are you ok?" asked Kannan.

"Yeah, I am ok," said Amma.

"There is something. Tell me."

"No. It's okay," she said.

"Tell me what the matter is?" Kannan insisted.

"No one asked me whether I wanted rose milk," said Amma.

Thinking of that moment, Kannan sipped the refresher he was having and coughed when a seed of the watermelon hit his throat in the last draw of the drink.

Kannan called Vaibhav and asked for the main course and went on to think.

"Mothers are like that, they never tell what they want. They hide their wishes for their children, even simple wishes. She could have asked that day but didn't. I still don't know the reason. She would be happy seeing a smile on her children's faces but would hide all her wants and needs."

Kannan quickly put his hands to his pockets and took the mobile phone out. Dialed the number and waited till it was answered, in a few rings.

"Hello," came the answer from Amma and Kannan could see the smile in his heart.

"How are you Amma? Finished dinner? Where is Appa?" asked Kannan.

"Yes, and Appa is watching his favorite serial on TV," replied Amma.

They talked for a few minutes and after the call was dropped the dinner was served before him, delicacies from far and wide, a special combo designed for him.

"Whatever be the cuisine, the smile which comes to my face when I walked out of Arul Jyothi with Appa's hand on my shoulder and the sad face of Amma not able to have the rose milk, priceless," Kannan thought.

He quickly took the phone and typed a message to Amma on WhatsApp.

"Amma, I'm coming home this Sunday. Ater the event, we will go for a movie and then a dinner at Arul Jyothi. And this time you should tell me what you want.Also a rose milk is pending from my side."

The phone buzzed a reply within a short while" :)"

5

It's raining

"Kanna, we will be back by 8.30, so take care and be a good boy," Amma gave Kannan instructions with a smile.

It was for the first time, Kannan was alone at home late. Kannan smiled back and felt pride in the fact that he is being given the responsibility to take care of the house. A bit of studies, bit of sun, and all the time alone at home. Though it was not a home alone story, Kannan waved a happy bye to Appa, Amma and Akka.

"Don't worry Amma. I will take care," Kannan replied like a grown up.

Kannan went to the gate and saw them get into the car and drive away. He ran back up home, locked the door and took the keys, started throwing and catching it in style and went straight to the TV room.

"Will watch TV for some time and then study," Kannan thought.

As Appa drove towards Swaminathan Mama's house, Amma started her usual doubts:

"Did I turn the gas off?"

"Did I switch the heater off?"

... and so on.

Appa and Akka heard a half and left the rest for her to voice and not be heard, as they were used to her doubts wherever they went, be it a day at the movies or a long distance vacation. These were common doubts in every mother's mind for sure and Amma was not an exception.

"Amma, Kannan is there and he will take care of it. Can you stop worrying?" said Pachai from the back seat.

"No. I think I left the gas main switch on," said Amma.

Appa and Pachai remained silent.

Meanwhile, Kannan switched the TV on and sat back in the chair like the boss of the house. In his black shorts and favorite blue and brown full sleeve t-shirt, he went to the mirror and had a look at the boss of the house for the evening. Combed back his hair and smiled at himself. Went back to his chair and watched TV for some time and then felt hunger creep up in his tummy.

The kitchen shelf was smiling at him with the yummy sweets Amma had made at home for Diwali. He ran to the kitchen shelf and took the whole big boxful of sweets. For a 12 year old boy, the whole house to his wish was more of a fun arena. He took a bottle of ice cold water and kept it near the chair. Sat on it with folded legs and kept the box in his lap like a baby. Opened the lid and started helping himself. Yummy ladoos, Puran Poli and all the delicacies smiled at him.

Each time he had a piece, he kept telling himself, "This is the last one," and had one more.

After a while, having had too much sweets Kannan felt a bit high in his head. Sweets can do it to you too. He switched

the TV off and went to his study. He opened the school bag
and took out his note books and placed them in front of him.

"Homework," Kannan decided.

He started with Maths, and then went on to English, and
then Geography. As he was writing he saw his handwriting
turn to wavy lines and not words. They made no sense to
him, neither would it make any sense to the Arundhathi
teacher, if she tries to read it the next day.

After the visit to Swaminathan Mama's house for
a function Appa was driving back home, when Amma
continued expressing her concerns.

"What would Kannan be doing? Hope he does not lock
the house from inside."

"He will be fine. Will you please stop worrying?" said
Appa in a stern voice, tired of the incessant questions for the
past three hours.

They reached home and saw the study on the first floor
and were relieved. Appa locked the car and Amma and
Pachai moved ahead. As Appa reached the door Amma was
ringing the bell and already looking worried.

"Listen. He is not opening the door."

Appa looked slightly worried and rang the bell again.
Akka's eyes started getting wet with tears, thinking what
would have happened to her little brother. Amma was
panicking and started calling out to the neighbors. People
started gathering and the knocks started getting louder and
louder. No one had a clue what was happening inside.

"Call Unni," Appa told Amma. "He can climb the wall
and reach out to the sunshade and open the window."

Amma ran to the next house to call Unni. Always ready
to help, he was a darling of the colony who would go any
length to help others. Unni was having his dinner when

Amma went to call him. Amma's voice shuddered as she called Unni.

"Unni... something has happened to Kannan. He is not opening the door."

He washed his hands and ran out with Amma in his lungi and a vest. He reached the door where almost the half of those who were awake in the colony to find out what had happened to the lovely little boy. Unni immediately jumped on the wall and climbed it. Swiftly he reached the sunshade. He tried to open the window and they were closed.

"Someone get me a screwdriver" shouted Unni.

Padmanabhan uncle who stayed in the next house sent his driver home to get the screwdriver from the tool box. Tool box was brought and the screwdriver was thrown to Unni, who was still on the sunshade near the window. He jagged the window open with a screwdriver and opened it.

"The fan is on, lights are on," Unni's commentary started.

"I can see the table and chair. No, Kannan is not on the chair," he continued.

"Check the floor. Is Kannan ok?" Appa asked Unni with concern.

"There he is. I think he is sleeping. He is on the books," said Unni which sent waves of relief to all waiting there.

"Kannan... Kannan..." Unni called getting no response from him.

"Someone get me a hose and connect it to the tap in the garden pipe," instructed Unni.

A long green hose was reeled out in rescue. The hose was connected to the tap and the other end reached out to Unni. The tap was opened and there it was, an artificial rain.

Kannan was in a dream world when he felt drops of water falling on him. He couldn't understand what was happening or where he was, when he woke up from the sweet slumber all the sweets had given him. He ran to the door and took the keys from his pocket and opened it. He saw a whole lot of people standing there in front of the door. The little boy with surprise in his eyes and seeing Appa, Amma and Akka standing with a whole lot of people he said.

"It's raining in the house."

Everyone laughed. Amma with tears in her eyes started laughing too. Appa was angry, and his anger fizzled out with the comment from Kannan. Akka was laughing out loud looking at the soaking wet Kannan. He got a grip of what had happened. His head went down with a smile and the realization. For many years to come Kannan was taunted in fun by all who were there.

"It's raining in the house."

Some memories are sweet and others sweeter. Every time water drops fell on Kannan's face, he would remember the episode at home when it was raining inside the house.

6

The little squirrel, Kannan

Kannan woke up to a lot of noise. He walked down the steps to hear the voices clearly. It was Venki Mama, Swami Mama, and a few others who were with them. They were walking in with luggage and the he heard Asokan, the assistant from the hospital who was instructing a nurse.

"Careful... careful. Hold her still. Let me close the door."

Kannan saw Ammamma being helped to get out of the car. The house was full of people. Amma was busy taking care of them. There was an air of tension and concern everywhere. Venki mama was trying to get the medicines from the bag from those kept in the corner of the room, Swami Mama was trying to get the bed ready. He was getting the pillow to support, the sheets to change and the blanket to keep her warm. All that Kannan knew was that Amma was taking care of Ammamma and she was home for treatment. She was not well.

Kannan peeped into the guest room where Amma helped Ammamma to bed. She was not looking as she used to. She was not laughing, smiling or singing as Kannan had seen her all these days. The shining face with the radiant smile that Kannan knew was missing and instead he saw a pain-stricken face. The smiles were missing on the faces of Venki mama too. Kannan's heart was beating fast. Fast with concern: What he can do to make her smile again. Or what else needs to be done. He was running around like the squirrel who wanted to do his bit for Lord Ram when the bridge across the ocean was being built by the monkey brigade.

Kannan heard Ammamma's frail voice. It did not have the energy as he knew she had.

"I am feeling...thirsty," said Ammamma.

"Ok, I will get you water," said Amma.

But she was trying to get things organized in the room and also had to accommodate Venki Mama and Swami Mama. Little Kannan, in his red stretch shorts and chequered shirt, had the sleepy morning face covered in concern, thinking what he can do for Ammamma to be alright. He rushed to the bedside. Held the lifeless arm of Ammamma. The hands that served so many with all the delicacies of the world remain motionless. There was a tear in his eye, which was waiting to flow off his eyes down the cheeks. His worry was so evident in the eyes. Ammamma saw Kannan and tried to smile. The smile hardly reached the lips when a tear rolled down the eyes of the grandmother and grandson.

"When will you be alright Ammamma," Kannan asked innocently.

Ammamma said nothing but smiled. Kannan saw her dry lips trying to say something. Dry as an arid land Ammamma said a few words which Kannan barely could hear her. But he understood that she wanted to ask how he was and talk to him to see him smile. Kannan saw her lips sticking to each other and and felt her love in the unsaid words. He thought for a moment and dropped the hand he was holding and ran to the kitchen.

"Where is Kannan?" asked Amma to Venki Mama.

"He was here a minute ago."

Kannan pulled the stool in the kitchen and opened the kitchen cabinet after climbing on to the kitchen worktop. He searched for something and heard Amma ask Venki Mama. He took the white container and climbed down. Pulled the stool towards the gas stove and took the black vessel with a handle and switched the gas stove on. Clicked the lighter and was up to something.

Amma was busy with her brothers, and suddenly heard a cry from the kitchen. A loud scream... and yes it was Kannan. Amma rushed along with Venki Mama and Swami Mama to the kitchen, where the scream came from. Ammamma wanted to get up and run as the scream seemed to pierce her ears and enter the heart, but could not. Amma saw Kannan on the floor writhing in pain with hands covering his eyes. He had not stopped crying. Venki Mama rushed forward and lifted the little boy in his arms and ran out of the house towards the clinic. He did not bother to wear his footwear nor was he concerned about what was happening all round him. Amma ran behind Venki. Swami Mama was perplexed but rushed back to Ammamma's room and started pacifying her.

"It's nothing, they have gone to the clinic... you don't worry," said Swami Mama to Ammamma.

The tension in their face was evident as Dr. Varma, Ophthalmologist rushed into the room and started trying to pull the little hands which kept the eyes covered. Somehow he managed to move the hand from the right eye, which was the one bleeding along with the tears. The nurse dabbed with cotton to wipe off the tears mixed with blood. The eyes had turned red and Kannan wouldn't stop crying. The doctor took his black gadget and looked into the eye carefully when the crying was slowly ebbing away. The loud screams died down to tiny sobs. He took a tiny forceps and carefully pulled out a whole cumin seed from inside the eye very next to the pupil. He took medicated drops and poured a drop into the eye. Kannan stopped crying, but the weeps were inside him.

Doctor turned to Amma and gave her the cumin seed from the forceps and smiled.

"It's okay. He is very lucky" said the doctor "Nothing to worry at all."

Amma let out a sigh of relief. Venki Mama smiled at Kannan. Kannan smiled back, wiping his tears mixed with blood with his shoulder, on the shirt.

"Don't touch or rub your eyes ok?" said the doctor to Kannan.

Kannan smiled wiping his nose with his hand.

As they walked back home, neither Amma nor Venki Mama asked him any question. Kannan was silent too. After walking a few steps, he spread his arms wide and wanted Amma to pick him up. Amma lifted him with all the love and walked hugging him, with his head resting on his shoulders. Amma and Ammamma had by then prayed with offerings to at least a dozen temples for his safety. Amma took Kannan to the bedroom, switched the fan on and carefully put Kannan to bed. The exhaustion put Kannan to sleep for some time.

He woke up to Amma sitting next to him and Appa was looking at him from near the bed. Kannan smile.

"What were you doing in the kitchen?" Appa asked softly and caringly. Kannan could sense the concern and love in his voice.

"Ammamma wanted water to drink and I have heard from Periyamma that water with cumin is good for thirst. I was trying to make some for Ammamma. I roasted the cumin and blew it and don't know how it went into my eyes," Kannan narrated his mistake with eyes wide open and the right one still red with the seed attack.

Appa ran his fingers through the hair and smiled. Amma was smiling at him too.

"Did you give Ammamma water? She was thirsty."

Amma smiled and shook her head in affirmation and said, "Little squirrel building the bridge for Lord Rama…"

7

Obsessions

"Good evening," said Kannan and waved at the security of the building as he drove the car into his parking. The exchange of smiles was friendly and warm. Every time Kannan saw him he would wave and smile. This was a practice which started after once Kannan saw Kevin, the security guy a little grumpy.

"What happened?Don't you smile?"

Kannan looked at the tall, Kenyan with white well-pressed shirt with the logo of the security company, trim blue trousers and a black shining belt with a silver buckle. He seemed never to smile.

"No. I am security. I have a serious job," was his reply in a typical African accent.

Kannan smiled back and said, "I understand your job is serious Kevin, but you can smile to me. I won't tell anyone," Kannan winked and added "It's our secret."

He gently smiled and as the car moved by him. He waved his hand and said *Hakuna Matata*

And since then there were no worries but smiles on his face. Every time they pass by each other they would greet with a smile.

The day was very long and started too early when the sky was being graded with brighter colors on one end of the horizon whereas the higher the sky went, the darker it remained. The day went on erasing the night's dark shades till dusk when Kannan was returning when the covers were up for the evening.

"You look tired," asked Kevin, the smiling security man who greeted with a *Habariako Mazuri Sana*.

"*Jambo Mambo* Kevin," said Kannan as he got out of the car with his Camera bag. "Was out to shoot nature and the heat shot me throughout the day."

Kevin ran to Kannan and took the bag from him and held his arm and took him towards the lift.

"You should drink a loth of wather," said Kevin and smiled.

With a smile on the tired face, Kannan waved Kevin good night and went to his apartment. The cool home welcomed him with arms wide open. Kannan carelessly threw his jacket on the sofa, removed his watch and placed it on the table and started removing the rings on his fingers.

That one is the navaratna ring - nine precious stones representing the nine planets.

That's the snake ring he bought from Nepal.

That one was Amma's gift and Kannan wanted a bigger snake ring than the previous one with the eyes of hessonite.

That one is a prayer ring – holy.

That one was a gift from his friend, for good luck.

The rings were not for superstitions, he just loved wearing them. Not one but six of them. That's what obsession does for any man. Kannan was no different. There are a few things which Kannan has been obsessed about since childhood. Like any young boy, he also aspired initially to be a truck driver, then a train coach driver and once he started seeing aircrafts fly high, he also wanted to a pilot. But these were not the three obsessions.

He loved taking pictures and camera became his first love. Appa had a Click III camera, a company which has been closed long ago, the contemporary of Agfa and Olympus. It was a 120 mm film, with manual forward clicks, without flash. It would need scorching sun to get a clear picture. Still Kannan was hooked on to it till he got a Konica Pop 10 camera when he was 15. The passion has given him a collection of different cameras today and the love still remains.

He loved reading, and books became a world of his own and last but not the least he loved rings in his fingers. As a young boy Kannan was always fascinated by the red coral ring in Appa's ring finger. He never removed it, unless when Kannan would carefully remove while Appa is asleep on Sunday afternoons. The young mind of Kannan always thought of that particular ring as a symbol of power or something that only Appa has. He would keep looking at the Gold ring with an oval red Coral in the middle and small gold florets done around it.

Appa was half asleep after Sunday lunch and young Kannan was on the ring as usual.

"Appa.... can I have this ring when I grow up?"

"Hmm."

Tell me Appa, can I have this ring when I grow big?"

"Hmm..." Appa responded in sleep.

"Appa..." Kannan shook Appa for an answer.

"Okay you can have it. I will get you one for your poonal (Upanayanam or the initiation thread ceremony)," said Appa.

Then the relevant and incessant question for the next few weeks was obvious "Appa, when is my poonal?"

And the day came when I was nine years and the invites were printed for the upanayanam of Chiranjeevi, Chi: for short, Kannan Iyer on February 26th of 1984. Kannan was not excited for the other reasons, neither social nor religious. He was excited that he would also have a coral ring like what Appa wears... the symbol of power. The functions were conducted in pomp and splendor like a wedding as it is one of the very important functions in life for the community. As the name signifies it is the upa nayanam or the opening of the mind's eye towards divinity, though no one understands it, and dub it as the day when a thread is worn to show that he is a Brahmin.

But the celebration in young Kannan's mind was looking at the small shining gold ring with a coral in the centre and similar floral design around it... just like Appa's ring. Kannan kept looking at it till he went to sleep and would start admiring it when he would wake up. The novelty remained till the day he went to Appa's nephew's wedding in Seergazhi in Tamil Nadu. The trip was long and tiring, but Kannan could not hold back the excitement in seeing all the sights all the way. By the time he reached the mandapam, everyone headed to the dining hall and wanted to quickly finish dinner and get some sleep before the next morning's function. The dinner time had slow buzzes of talks between the elders and there were the florist working on the decoration, the catering people cutting vegetables for the next day, there were a few serving dinner on one corner of the hall.

"Viswanathan, Gopal, Lakshmi, the function will start at 5 in the morning. So be ready," said Periathimbar, Appa's sister's husband, whose son was getting married the next day.

Kannan was walking back after washing his hands and shining the ring on his finger, saw Appa nod in the typical fashion which people say it's the style of Palakkad. He had his favorite Click II Camera dangling on his neck in a reddish brown leather bag, which cased the black compact camera. Both his loved possessions with him, he was the happiest boy in the mandapam.

"Appa, how is it?" asked Kannan showing his ring.

Appa smiled and said "Good, very good."

The travel had made everyone tired and were trying to get some sleep when in about an hour the whole mandapam was woken up by loud cries.

"That's Kannan" "That's Gopal's son", "Who is crying at this hour" those who heard started rushing towards the room.

There was already a crowd gathered inside the room. Kannan was soaked in tears and face had gone red.

"What happened?" those who stood around kept asking.

"Did he wake up seeing a nightmare?"

"It should be stomach ache."

"Did he fall?"

Questions started popping up.

"Give him some air please, "Appa said who was sitting next to the crying Kannan. The screams were getting loud when Appa replied "His ring is stuck in his finger. It's swollen, and the ring is stuck in his finger."

The small ring finger was as fat as the thumb by then and was turning blue. Kannan was writing in pain and was shouting as loud as possible. Probably the Guinness World Record Invigilators needed to be there so that he would have set a new record for shouting loud in the dead of the night. 15 minutes passed when a goldsmith was woken up from sleep by someone and he walked into the mandapam, where the cries and screams welcome him. He sat down next to Kannan and opened his small silver box. He was wearing a white shirt and dhoti with a frame like thick body and curly oil dripping hair. Even at that hour of the night the red kumkum on his forehead remained as is. He took out a small plier like device and took it towards Kannan's ring. The thought that the ring would be cut made Kannan scream louder, both in pain and grief. The plier worked and the screaming stopped. The ring was cut and the finger started turning pink again. For years, the marriage was referred to among relatives, as the one where Kannan's ring was cut in the night.

Kannan thought of that incident which he had heard from most of his relatives about how loud he screamed and smiled. The obsession for rings still remains. And so does clicking pictures. He quickly had a hot shower and came to bed and switched on the bed lights to be with his third obsession - reading till he slept for the night with all the sweet memories of the day and thought for a second.

"Am I obsessed with my memories?" but it made Kannan smile. So it's okay.

8

Smiles come back home

"Smile please," said Babu Uncle of Ensign Studio.

The studio was always a place of wonder for Kannan. He smiled at the amazing sights around him. Before the picture was clicked Kannan walked around the studio and the dressing room.He saw cameras of different kinds set to take pictures, the huge sheets of colored paper for the background. The red carpeted floor, the dressing room with a mirror and the smell of the orange and white tin of Cuticura powder kept on the dressing table by the mirror, the different combs and brushes, the coats and ties on the hanger on the wall, the huge reflectors and flashes of the studio floor; Kannan was lost in the world of photography. Kannan loved photography from a very young age and for the nine year old in his blue jeans, which he got from Jean Shack the previous day and well-pressed white and blue chequered shirt, stood prim proper with Amma in her violet saree and Akka in her blue and white frock with hair tied up in two pig tails on the sides.

"Click," the huge white umbrellas flashed a lightning and the photo was taken.

The picture was for Appa and that picture was very special with Amma and Akka. All that he understood then was that Appa has got a job in Nigeria and that he would be flying in an aero plane soon, with the smiling family picture. Appa was at the counter checking for the date when he would get his passport size photograph and the family photo. The evening was young and the next in line was dinner at Bharath Tourist Home, a restaurant which they went for celebrating special occasions or weekend eat outs.

As the dinner started Kannan heard Appa talk to Amma. While having the dosa silently he heard his words.

"They say I will have to fly in two weeks," said Appa.

"And how will you manage?" Amma asked.

"Will have to and you three can come after two years," Appa replied.

The silence after that statement said it all. It was for the better prospects of the family, but the separation was painful. There were no many smiles during the dinner. The aroma of the food did not lure the heart, nor did it make a difference as it usually did. The silence followed them till all slept that night.

Kannan opened his eyes the next day to see Appa get ready to go to office. He got up from the bed and ran to Appa and hugged him, holding the leg as it was the pillar of his love that he would not leave even at the cost of his life. Appa smiled and gave a pat on his cheeks.

"Chandu... Kanna... Good morning," Appa said with love.

Kannan smiled and asked, "Appa... are you going to foreign"

"Yes Kanna. And you will come too. Soon," said Appa.

The smile was slowly melting away to sad stares. The thought of being away from Appa was hurting Kannan for sure. The whole day at office Gopal, Kannan's Appa, found it difficult to forget the eyes which were looking at him in the morning when Kannan asked about his trip. Around 3pm he received a call.

"Gopal sir, call for you," said the receptionist and transferred the call.

"Hello," said Appa.

"Mr. Gopal, you have to pay 30,000 for the visa and associated expenses."

"Ok," said Appa and continued, "When should I make the payment."

"A week's time. Thank you."

As a matter of fact 30,000 was big money then, but it was not so difficult for him. The money was arranged in two days time. The list for purchase was made and home was more of silence than celebrations of the new avenue. Every day was mechanical as days nudged towards the day when the payment was to be made. More of sleepless nights for Appa and Amma.

Appa reached office and dialed the number of the agent who was making arrangement for the placement. All procedures of interviews and forms to be filled were done and it was the agent on the other end of the call.

"I am not interested," said Appa to the agent.

He came back home that evening with a smile on his face. He hugged Kannan who ran to him as he came back home.

"You are so happy. What happened?" Amma asked.

"Yes. I said no to the agent, I am not going."

Smiles returned home that evening as the heart filled with hopes of being together and not being separated from the family. Appa's life was completely for the three most precious people in his life - His family. Kannan, Pachai will have their Appa close to them. Amma smiled with a sigh of relief that they need not think about being away from him. Life is a choice we make as we live each day. And the choice Appa made between more money and more love was obvious. He chose love .... That choice would forever remain a lesson for Kannan when he grows up, and the picture they took at Ensign Studio will remind him of the same.

9

Indelible scars

Evenings were busy as always till Appa arrived. Little Kannan has his own ways of spending time. At times it would be carving a writing chalk, writing or sometimes painting. Kitchen used to be the bustle of activities where Amma was preparing the evening snacks and dinner. That was the time Pachai, Kannan's elder sister would always be with Amma sharing her day. That evening Kannan was busy with his work in his room when Akka was sharing the day with Amma. From everything that happened since she left in the morning. Kannan heard Akka cry to Amma and that caught his attention. He slowly walked towards the kitchen door without making much noise. He stood there at the door listening to them without being seen.

"And she was mocking me and asked me what the mark was in my hand," Akka was talking to Amma with tears rolling down her cheeks and pointing at the red scratch mark in her right hand.

"It's ok." said Amma, calmly dropping the next puri into the hot oil.

The sizzle of the dough in oil was more silent than the sobs of Akka. Kannan was scared what might happen next as the marks on Akka's hands were the result of the fight that happened the previous evening. It was a silly fight over mixing up the books on her table, tearing a piece of her notebook for paper and those are things which she would never like. Fights were usual between Kannan and Akka and he was equipped with nails to fight the age of his elder sister. The nails had left a scratch on the white pale skin of Akka, which was the topic of discussion in the kitchen.

"Will Amma scold me or would it reach Appa?" Kannan thought, and continued to listen to the discussion inside the kitchen.

"But Amma, I did not tell her that Kannan and I had a fight," Akka continued with tears rolling down in cascade." I told her that the pet cat had scratched me while I tried to lift him."

"Don't worry," Amma said calmly, "He is a small boy. You are elder to him and you should take care of him. You go wash your face and study. Go dear."

Kannan felt choked in his throat.

"What have I done? I shouldn't have," Kannan thought.

He slowly walked away to his room sad. And sat there with his books and crafts around him. Nothing seemed to excite him as the grief was overwhelming that he was wrong and put her sister to such a situation. It was the realization that his actions put his beloved sister to shame and insult that made him more withdrawn. It was nothing big, but for the small mind to fathom the lightness of the situation, it was really difficult. He did not get out of his room for coffee that evening. The evening was silent without the usual fights or pranks.

"Kanna..." he heard his Akka's sweet voice, "Come for dinner. Quick."

There was love and affection in her voice. She seemed to have forgotten the incident after the discussion with Amma. A silent dinner, the night's sleep and the morning sun changed the little Kannan for sure. He was determined not to physically hurt his sister anymore.

Years passed, and the incident was just a lost note in the huge library of memories they shared. Kannan was on an official trip to the US. He finished his meetings and reached the Children's Hospital of Pittsburg, UPMC. The busy sidewalks and the parking were as stereotyped as any other busy city. He closely looked at the boards which read Main Entrance, Mid Campus Garage, Penn Garage, Research Center and a few others. He walked through the sliding glass doors of the main entrance. The air had the clean and sterile scent of medicines and disinfectants. He went to the reception and asked for Dr. Pachanayaki. He was meeting her after many years.

"The third room on the right," said the old staff on the reception who was busy attending to a whole lot of patients at the same time directing them to respective doctors.

Each step towards the room, Kannan was reminded of the discussion Akka had with Amma in the kitchen. He saw the board at a distance. The years of studies and work, he was proud of his Akka. She has lived all her life spent in studies and more studies alone. He remembered the days when he used to drop her to the college on his bike. The time they spent singing while the power went off. The small pleasures and times of togetherness and the silly fights they had.

"Dr. Pachanayaki A, MD - Paedeatric Endocrinologist"

And it seemed to move farther as he walked closer. He saw a familiar face walk out of the room; the spectacles and the doctor's coat, the steth in her hand and the same sweet smile. For a moment he saw the sister in her teens with two braids of long hair and in her school uniform standing next to Amma in the kitchen. The incident which changed him. The silly fight and the scar. The images of the discussion in the kitchen flashed his mind again and again.

"AhKann.a How was your day? You said you would be coming home," Akka said in her same sweet voice.

Time seemed to have made her voice more mature. He stood there smiling and not saying anything.

"Oh well it was hectic. I couldn't make it," he said with his much earned life's maturity.

Though they rarely talked over the phone owing to the mundane work and life they had, the talk seemed to start from where they had left years back before her marriage and relocation to the US. Pachai looked at his brother. He has grown so much. Looks much older. She thought to herself.

They walked to the cafe nearby while talking about many things that they had missed due to busy schedules and took the coffee to the typical round table with cozy couches around it. They sat down and sipped the coffee. She removed the long sleeved coat and put it carelessly on the back rest of the seat and placed the steth on the table. The red knitwear and the jeans never made her look elder to Kannan. She pushed the sleeve of her sweatshirt and sat down. Kannan looked at the pale white right hand of his Akka and saw no marks there... but his heart still had the scars left by the small scuffle between the little brother and her sister. He never discussed the hurt and kept it to himself.

He was calm outwardly with his heavy heart still telling him "I shouldn't have hurt her. She is my only sister. Akka might have forgotten it by now. So silly of me," Kannan thought to himself.

Someday the scar in the mind would be gone too. The bond was still there between them shared with a smile. The kid brother and sister still fight in dreams but love each other as long as time stands. In their hearts they are still the same: The two braids with the white ribbon with the school uniform, the red shorts and the loose t-shirt. Kannan and Pachai will be kids forever in the beautiful minds with no scars in the love they shared for each other.

10

Eyes, they speak

"Hello. Anandashram," the lady on the other side responded as Kannan called.

"Madam, Kannan here. Day after is Diwali and I would like to come with some crackers and have dinner with the children."

Kannan could feel the smile on the face of the matron as it was more of a regular affair whenever Kannan was in town.

"Sure. How many of you would be there?"

"Three or four of us, and how about ice creams for the children? Is it okay?" replied Kannan.

"Great. There would be around 40 of them," was the reply.

"Ok. Then," Kannan smiled and hung up.

Be it birthdays or cultural or religious, Kannan had a special way of celebrating those special days. Festivals had a very special place in Kannan's heart. Apart from the celebrations with the family, Kannan found more happiness in donating blood for those who are in need, or celebrating it with those not so privileged, at Anandashram, to have a celebration. It was Diwali and Kannan's celebration would not be complete without celebrations at Anandasharam with the children there. It was not an orphanage but a home for the underprivileged. Many children there, had both their parents alive but the economic conditions would not let them live together. The trust was taking care of them with the help from the affluent in the society who would give donations or used clothes or any material needs of the home.

Arrangements were made for the ice creams to be delivered in the evening, ensuring Diwali to be special again. Kannan reached the home for the children when the sun was setting and giving an amber hue to the skies...before it would turn dark to enjoy the spectacle of fire crackers. The whole city was still in the celebration of Diwali, crackers went off here and there giving the city a misty happiness with smoke and the smell of firecrackers and the sounds of the crackers, which was so very peculiar for Diwali. With eyes closed anyone could say that it was Diwali.

But the doors of the ashram lead to silence. There were no celebrations inside the narrow corridors or the open area inside. The dim walkways had the benches ready for the dinner, where on the ring of the bell, children would come and sit as per the discipline of the ashram. The lights were on, but dim, hiding the excitement of Diwali. Kannan stood there with arms wide open and two huge bags in his hands full of crackers for them. With his salt and pepper beard and long hair, the golden evening sky cast the golden yellow shade on him and he looked more like a Santa Claus who has come in disguise to celebrate Diwali. He was a package of love in long white kurta and khaki pants, soft canvas shoes and the smile on his face seeing the children washed with the fading sunlight. As soon as they saw Kannan, children of different ages ran to him as they knew it's time for celebrations.

The children did not have new dresses, as the privileged would have. They did not have the best of the best looks. But they had one thing in common. Their smiles and love in their eyes. They rushed to Kannan like a swarm of bees towards a flower. They wanted just a hug and a smile. That was their celebration. The feeling of being wanted, the feeling of being able to celebrate in their own simple ways. Kannan joined the children as one of them. The middle-aged man turned to be a kid with them, getting the crackers out of the bag, giving them boxes of sparkles to start off. Flower pots, rockets and all that could bring more smiles to the faces of the children came out of the bags as if it was a Pandora's box.

All but a little boy was standing away from the crowd. A light blue colored t-shirt dulled and out of size, which would have been from the lot which people donate once they feel it is not fresh enough to be worn, torn blue shorts which looked neatly washed but spoke its age, tanned skin but still shiny bright face, which had eyes that kept looking at Kannan with the other kids. His hair was well oiled and parted well, combed to perfection. The eyes seemed to be moist with tears but he was not crying. They had an element of sadness to them. The lips were wanting to say something but silent. Vishnu was standing near the benches in the corridor. The hands were holding the pillar of the verandah in a reverse hug, as if someone had tied him to the pillar. There was a mole on his cheek which was more a beauty spot, for his charming young looks. He seemed to be better than the characters in *Oliver Twist*, by Charles Dickens.

"Come Vishnu. Come," said Kannan

He ran towards Kannan as if he was waiting to hear those words from him. Over the years, every celebration at Anandashram, Vishnu and Kannan shared a special bond. A bond which has no name attached to it. Kannan took out a box of colored sparkles, took two and lit both. Handed one to Vishnu and lit the kept the other for himself. They both smiled with one hand hugging each other and the other holding the sparkle. The smile on Vishnu's face was brighter than the burning sparkle.

There was fun, dancing, singing and fireworks which changed the open spaces in the ashram to a festive ground. The sparkles had colors of joy bursting out with more life than it is when the same was at home. There was life inside the ashram with Diwali. The noise, smoke and the joyful screams of excitement settled in a while. It was dinner time, and all sat down on the old wooden benches. Smiles added more flavor to the food. The sweets brought more smiles to the children. The ice-cream cups were cups of joy for them. The skies were being lit up by the crackers all around. Those were the colors of love as Kannan and Vishnu watched them together. Kannan was watching the skies when he felt a hand pat on his legs. Vishnu standing there, and it was his slender hands.

"Can I sing a song for you, uncle?" asked Vishnu.

Kannan went on his knees to the young boy and hugged him and said, "Will you sing for me?"

He smiled and started singing a song from one of the recent movies.

Kanneer poovinte kavilil thalodi...

As he sang, the small face with a smile was at its best. Vishnu's eyes, Kannan could not stop looking at those eyes. Bright and wide open, there was a spark of happiness in it.

"The best spectacle for Diwali," Kannan thought for a second.

Finishing the song, Vishnu stopped for a moment before everyone around him, all the children, the matron and every single soul applauded to appreciate the singing. The claps sounded like the best crackers for Diwali ever. Kannan still on his knees couldn't stop himself from hugging Vishnu.

"Uncle," Vishnu called as Kannan was getting up.

"Yes Vishnu?" Kannan leaned down to the little boy.

"I don't want to go home for holiday. will you tell the matron aunty?" pleaded Vishnu.

"Why? why don't you want to go home?" asked Kannan caringly.

"My Acha (Malayalam for father) is bad. he beats my amma (Malayalam for mother). He beats me too. He is bad."

The words after that pierced Kannan's heart, Vishnu's prayer wishing his father dead. Too much for a child like Vishnu to say.

The celebration was over and Kannan was leaving. He saw Vishnu stand away from everyone in a corner and smile at him. He waved with his hands but felt as if his heart was bidding farewell to Kannan. His drive back home was with only one sight in mind. The eyes. Vishnu's bright eyes. The eyes which spoke volumes than the words he spoke. The joy in simple things which gave a sparkle in the eyes. The eyes that spoke so much. Even after reaching home Kannan could only hear Vishnu singing and see only those eyes. Kannan could never feel that the incident haunts him, but it never went away from his heart. After dinner at home when everyone in the city was still celebrating Diwali with the fireworks that remained Kannan sat down on his desk with the table lamp on. He opened the diary where he used to jot down once in a while. He wrote a few lines that came from his heart.

"I saw the eyes that spoke more than the lips. I saw the eyes which had tears but never let them out. I saw the eyes and learned something new. That I never gave a thought till date.

"Eyes. They are with us throughout our lives, the mother's eyes that fill with tears of joy seeing you smile, seeing you walk, seeing you grow, seeing you achieve, they speak without words, they make you think. The eyes of a father looking at what needs to be done for his children, the eyes that strain themselves to give the little happiness for his family, the eyes that look for the best for them. They communicate without languages, they love without saying. The eyes make us love, they express what is in the heart which the lips never reveal. The eyes of friends that always follow you to keep you safe. The eyes that never see what they don't want to see.The eyes have been a part of the world we see.

"The moments when I wake up to see Amma smiling with a coffee for me;

The moments on Sunday when my eyes see Appa coming back from walk;

The moments when Akka comes out of the airport and the eyes keep searching for me;

The moments when Ammamma could see no more;

The moments when her eyes went emotionless, leaving memories behind;

The sparkle in the eyes of Thatha when he prays every morning and night;

The moments of naughtiness in the eyes during childhood;

The eyes that wait to see your loved ones;

The moments of love in the eyes."

Thoughts kept taking Kannan to a different world, a world of vision with the eyes of the heart.

"See more... till you see no more," thus finished Kannan. The drop of tear which was gifted by Vishnu still rested on the corner of the eye. Kannan wiped it and closed his eyes for the night wishing to see happiness in the sad world the next morning.

11

Destination home

For many, journey is for a destination, but for Kannan journeys were destinations. If there was something that excited Kannan all his life, one of them would be travel. A time for himself to let himself loose in imagination, fly with the wind that gets his hair flying, the people around him, the new lands, new languages, new people and each journey giving him something to remember. The childhood was filled with the memories of the black steam engine with its snout sneezing huge clouds of smoke with the smell of charcoal. The railway stations were a sight to remember. As a child Kannan was fascinated by how the red shirt wearing uncles, porters, could carry so many trunks, bags and boxes all at once, the smell of the hot vadas in the station and the small cups of hot coffee.

The visit to the book store at the station, the fresh smell of the books which always took Kannan to a different world. As soon as he got a new book, the first thing would be smelling the pages - something only those who have tried it before could tell. The strange gadgets with red and blue lights and a red and white striped disc which would stop rotating indicating the time to drop a coin when standing on it to get a small card with the weight on it and the reverse to hold a forecast for the day. Till his late teens the weighing machine at the station was more of a ritual where he would need the small shining silvery coin slipped into the slot to get the weight card. Kannan kept a whole lot of such weight cards and railway tickets for a very long time, till he lost them all in transit or misplaced it except from his mind.

Kannan learnt a lot from trains. They were moving institutions. Debates with other passengers, sharing a cup of the murky waters called coffee, the bread omelette in the mornings, the packed lunches and the way to adjust oneself to the tiny space called the berth in a position that looked similar to the child before the childbirth, shrouded into the space for a nap. The fans which never moved, springing to life with the edge of a comp tapping on the leaf through the rusty grills, the singers who would sing their own tunes to the very famous numbers popular for that time. The later part of his teens, trains and buses were more ofme time providers, the more he traveled he fell in love with the journeys.

Many trips during childhood were the six hour long fun time from Ernakulam to Trivandrum. Looking at old uncles and aunties sleeping while sitting, young uncles looking at young girls without being seen, the ones who tried to hide their face behind the newspaper as if their life depended on what was on the newspapers, all were intriguing sights. The regular journey towards Trivandrum always passed through Amma's college.

"This is the college where Amma studied," she would point out to the red bricked building with white shades by the side of the tracks as the train approached the station.

As soon as she would say that no matter if it is for the 100th time, Kannan and Akka who always fought for the window seat would stick their heads to see the college as if it were a family monument. That became a regular sight. Once during such a journey Amma missed saying the oft repeated lines. There was silence and Kannan and Akka were busy in their comic, they had got from the book store. A person sitting next to them quickly asked:

"Are you not showing the college to the kids this time"

Amma, Kannan and Akka had a hearty laugh the laughs remained in Kannan's mind for a very long time and every time the train would pass the college Kannan would remember the funny incident.

It was April of 2002 and a special assignment for Kannan - to emcee a mega event in Chennai. The tickets were booked by the organizers and he had everything packed in order. He reached the station and boarded the ac coach. The attendant, in his dull blue uniform, smiled at him and greeted, knowing that he would get some tips from each person in the compartment.

"Welcome sir. Which seat?" he asked with a smile which would attract a toothpaste ad, as it needed cleaning badly.

"AC3 24," said Kannan and smiled back.

He reached his seat and kept his bags on the upper berth for the time being. He removed the sling bag and kept it along with the luggage. Kannan remembered the ritualistic trip to the book store and needed a bottle of water. He instructed the attendant that he would back in a minute and rushed to the book store. Somehow he managed to pick a novel and a magazine and a bottle of water from the convenience store next to the bookstore and rushed back to the compartment. He sat on his seat and wanted to check the printed material which was in the black sling bag which he had kept along with the other bags. For his shock surprise and all the wonder that bag was missing.

"Did anyone see a bag? I had kept it there," Kannan asked everyone sitting in the nearby seats frantically.

"Did you see my bag?" he kept asking.

By then the train had started moving. Kannan's heart sank, as the bag had his passport, new shoes, more important as he wouldn't get his size anywhere and had got it made to order for the function, money, tickets and all the important documents for the function.

He ran to the door and banged it open with his body and went to the attendant

"Did you see my bag?"

There was not even an answer from him, just a shake of his hand gesturing an affirmative "NO"

He saw the Train Ticket Examiner with a dark face, darker than the black jacket he was wearing, with pan in his mouth and shell-frame glasses, who walked out to Kannan and asked.

"What is the praablam" in a mix of Tamil and English.

"Sir someone stole my bag and all my documents were in it, even the tickets."

"I know. People like you have all the excuses of the world, I can't do anything. Get down at the next station," said the TTE.

"But sir you can check the list. AC3 24 is booked in my name."

"That all I don't know. You show the ticket, or I put fine or you can get down at next station."

Kannan searched his bags and pockets for all the money he had and paid for the fine. Somehow with the worry in his head Kannan reached Chennai. All his documents and ID cards were gone. The next two days went in worry and finished the show to the best possible. By then he had arranged the tickets for the return as they were also in the lost sling bag. The event got over and Kannan had to reach the railway station in an hour's time. It was peak traffic and Kannan somehow reached the station exactly on time.

Kannan paid for the cab and rushed to the platform where he had to board the train. He ran through all the rush of the Chennai central. People where sleeping on the floor with luggage, there were vendors moving around the other trying to get to their trains. Kannan ran and jumped over people and boxes to reach the platform, where all that he saw was the train move away and the last compartment the signal staff was waving the green flag. He tried to run, but all in vain.

The pleasure of the onward and the return journey went down the drains. The success of the event did not give him enough happiness to cover the failure to catch the train.

With all the dismay in being late, he went to the information counter and got the cancellation form, but got a meagre amount as reimbursement as he missed the train and the train had already left. With all that remained with him Kannan got a train to Alleppy instead of Trivandrum and the train was full. With no reservation and the compartment full with people, Kannan experienced a new kind of journey, in an unreserved compartment by the side of the door and the lavatory with the vendors. His destination was for the first time was 'home' and forgot to enjoy the trip. But Kannan never forgot the journey.

He saw the life of the underprivileged, with no air-condition or fans, no seat or berth, all but a newspaper to sit on and spend the night without a wink of the eye by the smelly walkway till he reached Ernakulam. He opened the door and stood holding the railings for support. Wind washed him with the night's cold. With the wind in his hair, he ran his fingers through them and took a deep breath. He saw the night sky and the houses far with lights switched on, the night crickets made the noise typical to the region. He was tired but started coming to terms with the journey of a different kind. He kept thinking about all the journeys he had made and started loving this one too.

He broke the journey and decided to continue his trip back home at least after a few hours of sleep. Every journey is an experience, good or bad, it teaches you something new. Kannan stretched himself to sleep in the waiting room securely chaining with the baggage he had to the leg of the chair. He woke up in a few hours and got the tickets to board the afternoon train from Ernakulam Junction to Trivandrum. As usual he checked his weight and smiled at the fortune card which said, "Life is a journey. Enjoy it. You will have new experiences."

He went to the book store and got one of his favorite author Robin Cook's noveland boarded the train. There were uncles and aunties and teens and girls with their usual antics. By the evening the train was approaching Trivandrum. As the train passed the college, where Amma studied, reminded of the funny incident, he laughed again, and the smile remained till he reached home.

12

The man who met God

"Have you seen God?"

A huge discourse was underway when the question was asked by the main speaker, Swami Brahmanand. Everyone was silent and Swamiji with his saffron robes long white hair and fluffy cotton-like beard and the long strands of rudraksh beads around his neck gave him a typical saintly look. But he had a glow in his face, which was unique. The gentle smile while he spoke, the profound voice as if he was ordained to speak to all by Gods wish gave him an edge over the similar looking others in many ways. His hands moved as if it were music while he spoke. They seemed to have the touch which might give you the peace you are looking for. And the silence which ensued the question, was disturbing. He asked again:

"Have you seen God?"

The front row of VIPs looked at each other again as if they were confused. With all the faith a small boy stood up with his hands raised:

"Yes," said the boy.

"And may I know where?" asked Swami Brahmanand.

"In the temple, yesterday," was the innocent answer from him.

Swamiji smiled and slowly gestured the boy to sit down and asked again:

"Anyone else?"

"I have," came the answer from an elderly man, who was standing near the crowded sides of the hall.

"Yes, my son," said Swamiji, "And where was it and when was it?" he asked.

Sreerenganathan, the elderly gentleman was a man with a strong faith. His life revolved around the faith he had in God. A simple question, which many don't have an answer, pulled him from the crowd as a person who has seen God. Swamiji waved him to come towards the stage. There were many who wanted to get a glimpse of the Swamiji for his fame was not limited to India but far and wide. Sreeranganathan was wearing a light blue half sleeve shirt and a white dhoti, simple as his ways of life. His grey hair was well combed and was sticking together as it were gelled. People looked at his face which stood out from the rest with his long nose and bright grey eyes. The broad forehead had the crimson prasad. On his milky white smiling face, the prasad was speaking volumes about his faith. He walked towards the stage where Swamiji was behind the podium. The lamp on the side which had the five flames lit for the evening function, the agarbathi near its foot with the smell of flowers, the aura of the Swamiji gave a special temple like feel to the stage. Sreeranganathan removed his old leather chappals near the steps which lead to the stage and climbed up. Swamiji ushered him to share the experience with just smiles and gestures. He stood with hands folded like an obedient student ready to listen to the teacher, who was the teacher for the evening. Sreeranganathan walked towards the podium and the microphone with a smile, which gave out the confidence and conviction he had.

"Namaste. I am Sreeranganathan and yes, I have met God. *Ente amma* (My mother)...my Chottanikkara amma.... in my life Swamiji," said Sreeranganathan to the jam-packed audience. There was a slight shiver in his voice, but his faith was so strong and he spoke from the heart. He narrated the incident starting with eyes closed as in a prayer.

It was a Friday, the Makam day a few years back, and was on a pilgrimage to the famous Chottinakkara temple. I had just enough money to get me the tickets for my journey. I thought no further as it was a golden chance for me to visit Amma again. I reached the temple at around 7.30 in the morning and was so delighted having reached Amma's abode. I was at the temple that stands out to be a testimonial for the vishwakarma sthapathis. Where Amma is worshipped in three different forms, Saraswati in the morning, draped in white; as Lakshmi at noon, draped in red and as Durga in the evening, decked in blue. The temple where Guruthi pooja is performed for the betterment of the people. I was there to ask for Amma's help for my condition. To help me with my life. A help to bear the struggles of daily life. I am sure that she takes care of me still.

The morning summer sun was hot and I entered the temple and finished the darshan of Melkkavu Bhagavathy. The rush was more than usual and drained the energy out of me. But the moment I saw Amma decked in the white saree, I forgot everything. I forgot that I had not had anything since the previous day's lunch. I forgot hunger, tiredness, thirst, I forgot myself.

The people listening were on the edge of the seats, as it was about faith and there stood a man who claims to have met the Goddess. Questions crept into each one's minds: Where would have he seen Amma?

And Sreeranganathan continued.

With the happiness in my mind I walked out of the sanctum sanctorum. I was on my way to the Keezhkkaavu. The premises of the temple were filled with people from far and wide. Therewere the possessed waiting for Amma's blessings writhing in agony. Some were exhausted from the trance and had fainted and were on the floor on my way to the Keezhkaavu. I walked out of the huge canopy on the huge pillars and walked on the hot stone path towards the steps which led to the keezhkkavu. I felt I was about to faint. It was the hunger which I had forgotten. I could not walk a step more. I was sure to fall on the pathway. I somehow held myself and sat down on the steps. My heart called out to Amma.

"Amma.... I am so happy that I could see you again."

I felt a cold hand on my sweating shoulders. I wiped my face with the shirt which was in my hand and looked to side where I felt the hand. There was a small girl wearing a dhoti. She should have been 4 years or so, not more. Her eyes were like precious black stones. Her smile was like the gleam of the sun's rays on the still waters. He face was glowing and had something divine about her. She was wearing a thin gold chain which was barely visible on her sandal would like skin. She was as fragrant as fresh flowers in a garden.

"Grandpa," she called me. I could barely see her anymore as I felt I was fainting, and the sun was shining behind her head.

"Grandpa, you should be hungry. Have this banana. You will be alright," the child said in the sweetest voice I have ever heard.

I took the two bananas in a plantain leaf with some prasad in it from the small hands of the child. I could feel the cool hands touch my palms when she gave me the prasad. I had the first banana and went on to have the second one too. The sweetness of the banana was never so ever before. I finished the second one and looked around to thank the little girl. She was nowhere to be seen. Where were her parents I thought? Why did she give me the prasad? I was feeling as if I was not tired at all. I was rejuvenated. I had all the energy in me. I quickly rushed towards the main temple with all the might I had. The child was nowhere to be seen. I saw the picture of Amma framed on one of the pillars. It was Amma herself. She had come to give me food. She was there to give me the prasad.

As he finished with a trembling voice, his grey eyes were full of tears and started flowing like a cascade of gratitude. Sreeranganathan closed his eyes and folded his hands in prayer.

Swami Brahmananda's eyes were wet too. He was smiling with the moist eyes and spread his arms wide and hugged Sreeranganathan. Touched his head and blessed him and walked back to the podium. "God reaches out to you when you are in need. It need not be in the form we think we would see," said Swamiji.

For Sreeranganathan, he could hear no more and walked his way through the crowd, where everyone was looking at him in awe. He walked out of the hall and he could hear the discourse continue through the speakers. Words about faith and belief, about divinity and spirituality.He walked his way out of the premises where there were a lot of vehicles and walked his way to the dimly lit night road. And no one knew that there goes a man who had met God.

Was it God?Or was it the act of godliness which made him feel so? For believers the little girl was God and for others it was a kind-hearted act of a child who saw an elderly man in distress and exhaustion. But yes, God resides in each and every one of us, it depends how we realize it or see it. Next time you meet God, you will know for sure that it was Him who came to help you in person.

13

What's cooking?

Kannan was an unconventional home chef - no measuring cups and no measuring spoons, it more of 'eye ball it' and adjust 'to taste'. It was time for his evening dinner cooking and thought of making it special for the evening. He searched the rack for onions, picked one, picked a few cloves of garlic from the shelf, took a piece of ginger and a stick of cinnamon. With a little water he ground it to a fine paste. As he emptied the paste on to a bowl to make way for the next paste of tomatoes, Kannan smiled to the different occasions where he was the little chef, with a touch of his own.

From the time he was the little apprentice to Ammamma and Amma in their respective kitchens he was given little chores in cooking which taught him to be fast and accommodative in the kitchen. Those initial lessons from Ammamma to make the yummy maladoos from broken channa and sugar with hot ghee. Kannan could still feel the heat in his hand when Ammamma had given him a small handful to roll it into his first ever sweet dish. He could smell the cardamom in it and the ghee when the sugar and flour came together. He would earn the sweet by working for it with Ammamma in her kitchen, or that's what he thought when Ammamma would pat his tiny shoulders which was just a handful for Ammamma and say:

"Wow. You made maladoo all by yourself? Here this is yours."

Kannan would bite into one when the sugary treat would melt away in his mouth. He would smell of the ghee, sugar and cardamom till Amma would see his face smeared with flour and force him to wash his face.

"You look like maladoo. Someone will eat you up. Come wash your face," would be Amma's comment.

It was Amma who taught him to make rava kesari and the tips and tricks to make it taste better. Since his first trial was successful, Kannan became the official kesari maker at home for poojas and small gatherings at home.

Though Amma would not directly appreciate Kannan and say how good it was, she would secretly take bowls filled with the kesari and rush to the neighbor's house and tell Leela Chechi.

"Kannan had made kesari today. However much I try, I don't get this consistency," she said with a smile, taking pride in his abilities.

"Even for Akka's engagement," Kannan thought.

While he sautéed the onion paste and got the tomatoes pureed, he went on smiling thinking about the day when his would be Athimbar (brother in law) had come home to see Akka.

"Pachai, today the marriage would be fixed as they taste my Kesari," Kannan had mockingly remarked while he happily got the Rava Kesari to its jelly like consistency.

"Did Pachai make it?" asked Akka's would be father in law Dr. Narayan.

"No, my thambi made it" Akka replied with a smile, which had the pride and naughtiness in it.

There were many instances when Kannan found happiness in cooking for the family. With a sigh, Kannan quickly blanched the palak and made it into a paste. The cooking went on with the dry masalas, chili powder and salt going into the sautéed onion paste and the tomato puree giving it body and flavor.

Kannan fondly remembered his office staff coming for dinner, when he had cooked Chinese, the many times he cooked pasta for friends, and went on to check the taste of the mix after adding the palak paste to the wok. There was a smile of satisfaction on his face and started getting the chapattis ready by the side. The baby potatoes were just done when he added them to the curry and gave the final touches. He added a blob of butter to garnish the bowl full of alu palak with the smell of jeera, cinnamon and the masalas, leaving his mouth to water.

The dinner was ready and he set the table with all his heart. He was the VIP and he was the butler for the night. He sat down with the steaming chapattis and curry in front of him. Smiled for a moment and was about to start when he remembered that he had not got the bottle of water. He opened the fridge and took the bottle of water when the phone rang.

"Rajesh School", the mobile buzzed with the picture on it.

Kannan kept the bottle on the table and answered the call.

"When? Oh... ok... ok. No, no. I will be there in ten minutes," said Kannan in a hurry and cut the call.

He quickly pulled over a t-shirt and jeans and walked out locking the door and rushed to attend to the emergency. Rolled his long hair to a pony tail while he got down the lift. Rushed to the car and started it in a hurry. As he drove towards the hospital where one of his friends was admitted, Kannan remembered the chapattis and curry on the table and smiled to himself

"There has been so many nights when Amma used to prepare the food with so much of love and care and I would return having food from outside and only say I had, and not even ask whether she had or not," Kannan thought.

"Chef indeed. Chefs cook, but don't get to taste them," Kannan stopped thinking about it, by the cafeteria and ordered, "One egg sandwich please."

14

Home care service

It was one of a very normal day when the sun rose to its usual brightness.The morning rush on the road was usual and the life's routine followed Kannan with work from morning. Breakfast was on the go and he did not take time to enjoy it, as time and tide waited for no man and Kannan was no exception. The rut caught everyone, and it had a pet name - "Life". With his usual calls, meeting and appointments, Kannan sailed through the first half of the day and was at a lunch meeting. The clients shook hands after the lunch was over and it seemed that food was more important than the meeting. At least some of the clients give more importance to food than work. Kannan walked to the parking lot, where his car was parked, and the sun was at its peak and heating up the day before moving out for a set. Kannan got inside the pre-heated car, which was more like an oven by then.

Somehow got the car started and the blast of AC cooled the interiors slowly but steadily. Kannan switched the radio to listen to some songs, which would cut the boredom of the drive in the hot sun. And it started playing like a soothing cool wind from the speakers in the car in Shankar Mahadevan's voice.

Main kabhi batlaata nahin... par andhere se darta hoon main maa...

His drive was not lonely anymore as his memories took the back seat and started taking him on the journey back to his childhood. Kannan was so scared of the darkness and could never face it. Amma knew about this and told Appa one night.

"Kannan is so scared of the darkness. I feelhe should sleep with us here and not in the other room."

Appa smiled and said, "He is growing up to a man.A man whom the world would be proud of.He is my son."

The discussion was short and did not reach Kannan's ears, but reached his life from the next day. Appa would come by the last train in the night around 10 and walk back home. As soon as he reached with the song on his lips and a smile on the face of the satisfaction of being back with his world, his family, he handed the keys to Kannan and said to his ten year old "man",

"So you will lock the gates from today," handling him the responsibility and the cure to his fear.

Kannan found it really hard to step into the darkness of the night. The whole surrounding was drenched in the darkness he feared. He had not seen the *Harry Potter* series to learn to fight the dark as even J. K. Rowling had not thought about the book then. Kannan saw a hundred dark images following him with every step into the night towards his seat of responsibility the lock on the gate just 20 feet away from the doorstep where he was standing. It was almost impossible for him to walk the distance and lock the gate.

The initial days he could hear the heart beat and it kept increasing as he locked the gates. He would run back with all the speed he had in his adrenalin back to his safe haven.

Days became weeks and weeks became months. The little boy was learning to live his fears till the day he turned back to see those dark images following him, and there were none. Just darkness of the night. Kannan smiled to himself. Appa's act of making him lock the gates gave him the strength to fight the fears. He was a bit bolder than the previous night. But the strength the ten year old boy gathered made Appa proud and Amma more worried later in his teens as he would be gone in his bike late in the night with no fear to tread the night.

The thoughts brought a smile to Kannan's face and the song to a close.

Tujhko sab hai pata…. hain na maaa…. and it faded. Kannan quickly switched the radio off and dialed the number from his phone; the number he remembered so well.And the picture flashed on his phone.

"Dialing Amma" with a picture of her smiling though to him.

"Kanna, was just thinking of you. How did you know?" Amma started with no pause with all her excitement.

"Where are you?" replied Kannan calmly with love in his voice for his dear Amma.

"I am at Coimbatore. Came here to drop Vijayam Aunty. She has rented out a house in a place for the old. The food is so nice, the area is so good, so calm, and there is a temple nearby and … and…" Amma's excitement was like that of a kid who had seen a toy of her choice.

"Hmmm …" Kannan continued listening to her.

"I think I should ask Appa to take a house here and come and settle here," said Amma.

It sent a thousand daggers to the heart of Kannan. "Have I left them so lonely that they have to check for options for the old? Have I not cared for them enough?"

The moments Amma was concerned that Kannan was afraid of something, the confidence in Appa's voice when he told someone Kannan would do it, the proud moments, the togetherness, the love, all took shape of daggers and reminded Kannan of the loneliness they are exposed to.

"Amma ... " called Kannan stopping her narrative about the garden and the river near the facility.

"Do you like to stay in a place like that?" Kannan asked with all the pain hidden in his heart.

"There is help on beck and call. We are getting old and its easy with a car we can visit the city too," the voice faded with the realization that her words had hurt her son somewhere.

"Just asked," Kannan said quickly and changed the topic. "So, when is the return?"

Amma smiled and replied, "Back home this evening."

The call ended but the train of thoughts did not stop. Kannan finished his days work and kept thinking about the day's events, more about the call.

A few days passed and Kannan sent a message to Amma.

Sending a person home today to take care of you both. He cooks well and will do the cleaning as well. He will take care of you and knows driving as well. I have told him about all that you need. Even the long drives on weekends to temples... Love Kannan

Amma's phone buzzed and she saw the message from her son. After reading it she turned to Appa and said, "I don't know who Kannan is sending. He should have asked. Will he stay here? How can he?" the list of questions as usual started one after the other to Appa. Appa was silent and was used to the endless list of questions. Amma's worries knew no bounds. She was trying to find a reason in her mind to send the person off, as she would not be comfortable with a third person at home all the time.

"He has not even said when the person would be coming. I have to go to the temple, then have to visit Venki. He had called," Amma was saying this when the bell rang. She stopped and walked towards the door with all the apprehension about the person who Kannan had sent. She opened the door.

"Home service for cooking and cleaning and taking care of you," said her smiling son Kannan.

The hug and the tears spoke volumes of the decision he had taken to be with them for good taking care of them from then on. Appa smiled as if he knew: He knew his son so well.

15

No more smoke

Kannan walked into his room and paused for a moment. Took a deep breath and it was the smell of fresh air mixed with the fragrance of incense in the room. The morning wash left a few drops of water in his salt and pepper beard which he wiped away with his palm. Tied up his lightly dried long hair trickling with water and wore the dhoti for prayers. The prayers gave him the strength to move on, and so it was his daily routine - 30 minutes to his God, up close and personal with him. The room felt more like a temple for him at that moment for sure. The bundle of white paper on the table and the file next to it which held the writings, which Kannan had finished last night lay there. The bed was kept properly with fresh sheets straight from the laundry. He sat on the black cushioned ottoman, his prayer seat, before the picture on the wall and started praying.

A few days back things were different, when he had not changed his routine as it is now. The day began with smoke and ended up in smoke and filled with more smoke every hour. The same table which had the sheets of clean white paper and pen, the sketch book and the spectacles, had more to hold. The table would be smeared with ash on the keyboard, ash on the headphones, ash on the books and notes and whatever lay on the table.... and not to mention the ashtray which resembled the Pandora's box, which was holding more cigarette buds than it could ever hold in them. Lighters could be found in every corner of the house. But all that changed so fast.

As his prayers finished, the room was filled with smoke but of the incense. The sunlight entered the room through the window and found its way to the clean carpet on the floor. The red carpet on the floor was new and the light gave it a new glow. Kannan walked towards the window the bright sunshine glow gave him a feel as if it was a hug from Appa. He saw the phone hooked on to the charger and stretched his arm and picked it up. Dialed his ever-familiar number or rather one of the last few numbers he knew by heart.

"Amma, how are you? Happy now?" Kannan asked.

It was a promise Kannan had given, but never kept for years. Every time Amma told Kannan about the ills of smoking, he would smile and say.

"I know ma, I will stop soon."

But the soon never came till date. There have been many days when he would stop smoking and start again. For those who tried to dissuade him from smoking would get intelligently woven stories of why he would not stop. There were times when his smoking would reduce in numbers but not take the final step of quitting. One or one pack, he would be still smoking. Those who knew Kannan would say... it's impossible for a person to stop Kannan from smoking as he knows it's bad and is okay with it. It was a few days back when Kannan just decided to quit smoking, which made

Amma proud and happy. Her happiness was that her son is getting back to life.

Amma still remembered the night. A few months after Priya had left Kannan for good. Kannan kept himself busy with work far and near and would return home late in the night. Kannan would rarely have food at home. The time Kannan walks in he would find Amma sitting in the front hall room where she would be holding on to a book but would have slept off reading it and the specs on her nose would have taken its position in the tummy by then, falling off the bridge in sleep. The sound of the door opening would wake her up and then would come the usual question.

"Dinner?" followed by the usual answer by Kannan, "No, I had."

Amma would clear the dining table after hearing the daily emphatic no from Kannan. He was getting into wrong company Amma thought, and so was he. The smell of smoke in his clothes and when he walked in was a testimony to him being in the wrong company. The same kid who fought with Venki Mama and Swami Mama to stop smoking and tell them the ills, ifs and buts of smoking, had started smoking.

It was well past two when Star Movies was playing on the small television in Kannan's room. *The Mask* was his favorite film and Kannan was watching it for the umpteenth time then. He lit a cigarette and puffed it out with a cough as it was the second one lit back to back, in chain reaction. As he let out the smoke into the air, the room smelt of tar, and smoke from the cigarette. He took another puff and the smoke when it mixed in the air, an image appeared from within the smoke. Someone standing at the door of his room. It was Amma. Kannan's heart sank as he never wanted Amma to see him destroy himself in smoke. She was worried about Appa, who still is a teetotaler, and what would he go through when he comes to know about his son being a smoker.

"Yes Amma" asked Kannan mechanically putting the butt of the cigarette into the ash tray.

"No. Just came to see whether you have slept or still awake," Amma replied.

Kannan could see Amma's eyes filled with tears. She said nothing more and walked away. The night went in guilt and tears for Kannan and as he woke up the next morning, he saw Amma pack her bags.

"Where are you going," asked Kannan surprised.

"Just... Just like that going to Ernakulam. Have some work there," said Amma and zipped her travel bag and walked away. Amma knew what Kannan was going through and did not have anything to say seeing him take a wrong path. That day remained in the minds of both Kannan and Amma. Years passed and from the light smoker Kannan started smoking more and more with the passing of each day.

On the morning Amma received the call Amma could not believe her earsbut loved to believe them for what they heard. It was Kannan's call. Amma had just finished her prayers and came and sat on the chair by the side of the dining table. The fan was at it full power and she heard the mobile ring. It was Kannan alright.

"Amma, I have a good news," said Kannan.

"What happened?" Amma asked out of curiosity.

"Amma, I gave up smoking," said Kannan followed by a big pause from both ends. Kannan could feel Amma's eyes fill up with tears when she remained silent.

In her hear she was thanking all the Gods she had been praying to. When, why, are you alright and so many other questions which were flooding Amma's mind, but she asked none.

The phone beeped the disconnection, and the disconnect in Amma's mind."So many years; what must have made him stop. Is he alright?" Amma was worried, but thankful to God for the decision. Amma had to ask but remained silent. It should have been Gods way to bring her son back to life, she thought. Kannan cut the call, and at that instant Amma rushed to the temple to thank all the divine forced behind the change of mind. Kannan looked at the pack of cigarette and the lighter on the table.

It was one of the days the previous week when Kannan was to visit an office for a client meeting. The green glass, the pots with ornamental plants, the wooden reception counter with a lady smiling and answering the calls and attending to the guests at the same time. From time to time she looked down. Kannan walked up to the reception to check the time of the meeting. She should be in her late twenties and was well groomed with one of the most beautiful smiles he had ever seen. Probably the secret to that smile was next to her. As he gave his card and waited, the lady looked down and there in a pram was a smiling young boy, with fair milky skin, soft silk like straight brown hair, dark eyes giving the bubbly kid the look of a doll or was it more divine than a doll. As his mother touched the boy and smiled, he started a spontaneous burst of smiles back to her. The reception was more a centre of joy as the whole place was filled with smells of baby cream, fresh flowers, fragrance of perfumes mild, yet catching the attention of the one standing there.

"I have an appointment with Mr. Rex," said Kannan without taking his eyes off the kid on the pram on the other side of the reception counter. As she checked the appointment schedule Kannan interrupted "Your kid?" while looking at the boy who was jumping with happiness and wanted to be picked up from the pram. He was so excited to cut himself loose from the bonding seat belts of the pram.

And she smiled "You will have to wait for a short while as Mr. Rex is on his way," said the brown eyed lady at the reception.

"Can I take him for a walk around the garden as Mr. Rex arrives?" Kannan asked without thinking whether it was appropriate or not.

"No, he is allergic to smoke," she replied.

And the gesture of her nose rubbing her fingers showed how strong the remnant odor of the smoke remained with him even after a while. All he wanted was to play with the bundle of joy, who wanted to be picked up and loved for a while, or that was what Kannan thought. But just a habit, which he had been stuck on to, denied him of a simple pleasure. Kannan choked as he saw the sights over and over again for a few nights and felt as if it was haunting him.

"A few days back a girl … no, a woman… should be an angel, or was it God's ways? The angelic child, denied to him over smoking."

The noise in his head was silenced by a scream from within, "I quit." And so he did.

Kannan had the pack of cigarettes in his hands still, looked at them for a while and threw it in the dust bin. Since then his room never had the smell of smoke, but of the incense he lit in front of the Gods. Kannan still smiles at the thought of the divine child in the reception area who made him quit smoking. The magical revelation, so to say, which changed his life forever. The smiles on his face would never be covered in smoke or tar. Kannan took a breath in and exhaled long. He felt peace enter his heart. No more smoke blurred his vision. Kannan looks forward to visit the office to just meet the little VIP in the pram by the reception desk.

16

A new name for the past - Fate

The setting sun seemed to be too tired with the day's events and just wants to plunge in the cool blue ocean lashing the sands and Kannan stood there watching the sun move fast into the arms of the ocean. The wind caressed his hair like a mother would do when she sees him worried. The heat of the day left a few drops of sweat which was being wiped by the evening beach winds. His eyes were wet yet tried to hide them as there were others watching the sunset. But they would be having something else and each one will have a different feeling looking at the sunset. Kids were flying kite and the kite had a shine on it like the dreams and hopes of tomorrow. Kannan was thinking of the time that was while he saw the speeding sun diving into the ocean.

Four years in college: The fun, the pain, the exams, the sessionals, the rough records, the workshops. Engineering was not the first choice for Kannan, but he seemed to enjoy it then. The companionship and camaraderie, the love and the silly fights and all that came along with it. It was for Amma and her alone, for her words were, "You get me the degree certificate and then do anything you want to do."

The initial days in college in the C1 batch of Civil Engineering students, Kannan was a loner. Probably the tall stature, huge and matured look, kept others away and Kannan was not in a mood to confront those issues. He would walk in and sit in the front bench and hide everyone behind him with his wall like body and gave them the freedom to pursue their antics. The seniors in college thought he was in his M.Tech or some other master's course because his size never gave him a look of a first year student. The UFO's (Unidentified Flying Objects) hurled from behind on Salim Sir who used to give sedative lectures on Economics, which put almost everyone to sleep, the exchange of film magazines, the discussions of girls about the new trends in churidars and accessories; all seemed not to be Kannan's cup of tea.

Kannan reached Vattakottai on his bike just to see another sunset as he watched with his friends in college 8 years back. The excursion to Vattakottai from college was to get acquainted to each other and spend the next 6 semesters together. But that trip changed Kannan's life. It was the day he spoke to his friends in his class. Kannan was sitting on the same ledge on the fortress where Priya, Jyothi and a few others approached him on that day.

"Are you Tamil?" asked Priya.

Kannan smiled and said "Yes."

"Oh me too," the 5 foot two stout girl with a white t-shirt with a picture of a sunset and huge brown shell frame shades over her big eyes, which covered her high cheek bones and a pony tail tied high replied.

"I am Priya. And you?"

"Kannan... Kannan Iyer," said Kannan.

"Bond ... James Bond" was the reply and they all laughed.

Though in the same class, they never communicated much. But very less they knew that the acquaintance was for the next 8 years. The next three and a half years in college changed the friendship towards support for each other. The time to share their studies, notes, thoughts, and difficulties.It was the end of college and time for them to decide what they should do further in life. They didand got married. The night before, on December 7th, there was so much of excitement. Kannan could hardly sleep. All night he was hushing on the phone about the next morning's arrangements. Got up early and had a quick wash and wore a white silk shirt and dhoti. Appa saw him in the strangest of morning wear and asked.

"What's special?"

"I am going to the temple after I drop you at the station," Kannan said with a smile.

Though he was telling the truth, it was not the whole truth. The results of his exams were not yet out and he was going to get married without letting anyone know. But a few friends who were a part of the plot. Probably that's why the oath at the court asks the witness to say the truth, the whole truth and nothing but the truth. Kannan was silent as the white Fiat KET 3080, moved steadily with Appa beside him to the railway station.

"I will be late," said Appa.Kannan nodded. He got out of the car and bent down as if to pick the coin he had dropped purposely and touched Appa's feet and said nothing. But his heart spoke a lot then. He needed his Appa's blessings.

He drove to Priya's house, where she was equally tensed. She was dressed simply in a green saree and a golden blouse. A simple chain on the neck and a couple of bangles as if it was just another temple visit. The moment they had been waiting for was just a couple of hours away. There were a thousand butterflies in his tummy. No one knew about the marriage except Priya, her parents, the one and only friend of her father Ramakrishnan, a few friends and Venki Mama.

Venki Mama was all so tense near the temple when they reached. He had ordered a tea and did not drink it. Instead he ordered a bottle of cool soda and did not have it. He did not know how Appa would react when he comes to know that he knew. It was more like Venki Mama was on the delivery table and he was about to give birth. The birth of a new chapter in Kannan's life.

The temple gave a feeling of being blessed by God. All were waiting for the moment. The lamps, the smell of the burning oil in the lamps, the incense and camphor, the garlands, the music on the speakers in the temple, the brass utensils and the December morning wind outside. The tension was ebbing off. The poojari came out from the sanctum sanctorum and gave the yellow thread well covered in turmeric as it is supposed to be sacred and auspicious with the gold medallion, which would be the sign of the marriage.

The wedding knot was tied in front of the deity. Venki Mama gave Kannan one of the white tube rose garlands with a red rose as decoration on it and the other to Priya. The garlands were exchanged without much pomp and splendor. There were no special band to play the wedding bells, but only the temple bells and a devotional song playing in the temple sound system. There were no special gatherings of people but just a few who witnessed. The fragrance of the garland filled their breath and their hearts with happiness amidst all the tension. Kannan and Priya stood there for a moment in silence with folded hands. The life changing moment. Two people who were friends at college now from then on were husband and wife. There was a moment of stillness, probably never before or never after. The rites at the temple were over and the husband and wife signed in the temple register. They lifted their heads, looked at each other and smiled, not knowing till when the smiles would last.

All four years of married life flashed in Kannan's mind. The starting of life together, being there for each other, working together for a while in one office, the quick lunch outings and the late night movies, the long bike trips, travelling to Hyderabad for further studies, their life and difficulties in Dubai and return, the long hours of work and not giving each other the quality time, the scuffles and fights and last but not the least, all the people who crept into the relation as mediators, soothsayers and problem solvers worsened or rather distanced the two. The flashes of thoughts were many - some sweet, some sour, some happy some painful, some of togetherness and some of being away. But it was a wild storm of thoughts indeed when others were enjoying the serene sunset.

"Here, take this," said Priya after one of the daily fights. Priya stood before Kannan with the medallion, the sign of marriage in a chain, in her hand. Threw it to the floor expressing her discord in the fight. Gone are the days when the insignia of marriage need be around the neck of the wife. It has now turned to be just a fashion accessory, which can be worn or removed as per convenience, at least the sentiments no longer exist in many. But this day marked the end.The end of all the decisions and thoughts. Ended so soon. What started with laughs ended in tears.

The smiling face in their mind were being taken over by the angry visages. Like leftover milk curdles over time, the relation too curdled with days passing. Kannan wiped his tears and a chapter ended in his life. Tears came to his eyes as the heart was stuffed with hurting memories of the past, as it was not usual for people to share their struggles with others with an obvious question in the end.

"What will they think?". Yes, men do cry. They do have tears to shed, but life is strange and has so much in store, but we never know what is around the corner. Kannan took a deep breath and exhaled the thoughts along with his breath. He kicked his 350 cc Bullet to a heartbeat and drove back with memories washed by the golden sea at Vattakottai. As he distanced from the beach, the sounds of the waves faded away and Kannan had made up his mind to move forward in life, leaving the broken dreams and memories there in the beach for the ebbing waves to wash away. The sense of adventure and happiness on December 8th was being replaced with scars of the wounds of life as memories. He drove into the darkness of the night full throttle giving the 8 years one name - fate.

17

Pictures from the past

For every mother it is hard to let their sons risk their lives, and for Amma, after the accident, every time Kannan gets on the bike, it is stressful. But for the love for his bike, Kannan would go to any length to fulfill his dream of going on a ride whenever possible. Letting go of all the thoughts and enjoying the ride. He would get up early tune his bike to his heart's desire to hear the heartbeats of the mate, his 350 CC Classic. On his usual shorts and t-shirt with a half helmet with his brushy beard, he looked so much out of place from what the localities usually see. Kannan mounted the bike and paddled the bike with his legs towards the gate when he saw Amma returning from the temple.

"Amma, I will be back soon. Going to click some pictures," said Kannan smiling.

The early morning sun had just spread his arms in a hug to the world and the slight drizzle the previous evening had moistened the ways Kannan was about to roll on with his Bullet. Amma smiled at Kannan's statement and carefully searched for the sandal paste in the banana leaf with flowers and a small sweet banana which she carried in her hands from the temple. She took the prasad and smeared a little sandal on Kannan's forehead and closed her eyes in prayers. The moments of silence and prayers seemed to be blessed by God with soothing winds enveloping them in divine grace. Amma's wet hair tied lightly behind after bath, had a few tulasi leaves on it. Her closed eyes opened and she took a little sandal paste and put on the headlight of the bike. Took the banana and gave it to Kannan.

"Drive safe. Don't speed Kanna," said Amma even when he was on his short ride this morning.

Kannan got off from the bike and touched Amma's feet. He always felt there is a bit of heaven under her feet. The prayers would be more important to him than any protective jackets or helmet. He walked back towards his bike, kicked it to start off a journey which he had been wanting to set out on for a very long time. As he moved slowly out of the gates he stopped and looked up. On the third-floor balcony Appa was standing to wave at him. Kannan smiled and waved at Appa who kept the steel tumbler of coffee on the ledge of the verandah and waved at him. With all the love prayer and blessings Kannan raised the bike to a full throttle. The change of gears and the speeding bike left behind Appa and Amma praying for his safe return soon.

He drove through the morning silent roads which extended limitlessly in front of him as every stop he made during this journey was a destination itself. Each one had a special place in his heart. Thinking of the childhood days when Appa would drive his white and green, KLR 6941 from Ernakulam to Trivandrum to Thatha's house.

He reached the old twin house in Trivandrum, not very far from where Appa and Amma stayed now. The house where he and Akka used to listen to stories from Thatha, the house where the kitchen was more a celebration each day with whatever it had mixed with loads and loads of love. The house where all the mamas and mamis lived together as a huge joint family.

Kannan saw the ISKCON temple opposite to the house where Natarajan Mama used to play the dhol during the evening bhajans. He also saw the remnants of an old shack, which used to be the shop where Thatha bought his betel leaves and supari for the night time pan for 20 paise, the small round copper coin which had a lotus engraved on it. Thatha used to call it Nagu's pan shop. Some days where more exciting when he got a chance to buy the small green menthol flavored sugar confectionery dearly called as *gas muttayi*.Four pieces for 10 paise, the fairly big flowery aluminum coin which no longer is seen with people as the smallest denomination these days are 5 rupees.

Kannan took out his camera and clicked the pictures of the old house which no longer was a home for the family but a store house of some trading company. These pictures will remind him of the good old childhood days. He could even see the green and white car parked outside and young Appa and Amma getting out of it with two kids himself and Akka in the back of his mind. The images were not dulled by the passing of time. He could hear Ammamma singing *Sreechakra raja simhaasaneswari sree lalithambikayae* ...(A devotional song).

As Kannan kept clicking pictures of the old house he could hear Ammamma call out from his heart.

"Kanna ...." and the child who yearned to hear the call ran out from his heart out to the gates of the house where Ammamma was standing with arms wide open to hug her grandson.

The well-combed hair rolled to a bun of the yesteryear fashion and the diamond nose pin in the shape of a peacock, the flower shaped diamond ear rings, the gold bangles, though less in number as she used to take one out bend it and give it to Venki Mama each time he needed money for something or the other, the fair glowing skin adorned with the beautiful smile filled with love, the smell of Exotica talcum powder, the peacock blue silk saree with a dark Prussian blue border and the shell frame glasses. Kannan's mentor in many ways, Ammamma was close to his heart. The deft hands once dishing sweets and all that he wished to eat, the filter coffee in the morning and evening, the aromatic pulinkari with leaves of the drumstick tree, the coconut chutney and soft cloud like fluffy idles in the shape of a full moon, all came to Kannan's mind.

She would make drums of coconut burfee for Kannan as he loved to eat them and would remain at the railway station till the train left. Kannan would keep waving at her till the train had moved really far. The young Kannan would try and peep out of the iron railed window to see if he can get a glimpse more of his Ammamma.

It was during his tenth standard that Ammamma left the world, leaving behind strong memories to all. She was a friend to all; a doting mother to her children, a loving grandmother to Kannan and Akka. Her long fight with diabetes and its difficulties all came to a stop. Those last one monthwas really hard for her. The glowing skin gave way to wrinkles the eyes that shined bright saw only darkness, the hands that made the delicacies moved no more and she was bedridden for years till her last breath.

It was after Thatha's death they moved to another house. Swaminathan Mama, his wife Jayam Mami and Venki Mama were the ones to take care of her during the last few years. One of those dark nights Venki Mama came home really late. He slept near Ammamma on the floor when she would try to get some sleep in the darkness her eyes gave her all the time. She would hear the TV shows as long as it played and imagine all that was happening and after which the only sounds she could hear was that of the ceiling fan whirring all night.

Well past 2 in the morning Venki Mama was woken up by a feeling in his leg. He felt a warm liquid wet his feet. Venki Mama got up and switched lights on to see a rat run away from the bed where Ammamma was sleeping. The rat had gnawed the motionless legs of Ammamma and blood was gushing from her wounded toe. The pool of blood was fed by the blood that was oozing from her toe, while she was asleep. The diabetes had numbed her limbs to an extent where she could hardly feel the pain, and doctors had warned about such difficulties even at an early stage. The only pain she had was that she had to seek help every need of hers. Venki Mama did not know what to do and frantically banged the doors of the room where Swaminathan Mama was sleeping.

"Swami... Swami ... come fast," that's all Venki Mama could say and they rushed her to the hospital on that morning of November 17th.

Kannan remembered the whole month when every evening he would be with Amma at the hospital and people came and visited Ammamma, knowing that she had not much time left with her. The hair which lived all the fashion of those days was now just a thin pig tail braided to keep her clean. Weakness overpowered her and hardly spoke a word or two. The drips, medicines and nursing went on and on trying to get her to normalcy. And after all the efforts by the doctors for over three weeks, she was stable and discharged on the 15th of December.

"That's all we can do for her," said the doctor while she was moved in the wheel chair to the car.

No one expected her to hold on to life so much. Even some prayed for her peaceful death seeing her suffer for so long. On the night of December 16, she woke up from sleep. It was almost ten in the night and Amma and Kannan were about to leave for home, when she called.

"Paappa," and Amma was shocked to hear the call. "Where is Venki?" she asked

Everyone rushed to the dimly lit room where she had spent many months in bed. She slowly pushed herself up with the partly paralyzed hands and sat up. The shock in the eyes of everyone there was evident.

"Appa is here. Even Mahadevan," she continued.

Amma's eyes filled with tears as Ammamma was seeing all those who had died.

"Lalitha has also come. I never thought I could see you all," Ammamma said in a frail voice and pointed to the empty corner of the room where maybe she saw her dead sister standing.

"It's just a dream. She is delirious," said Venki mama and helped her lie down and get back to sleep. "May be from the medicines," he added.

The flame which was burning bright all night went off the next morning in sleep. The void she left behind with her passing away, was still there in Kannan's heart. He mechanically closed the lens with the lens cover and put his camera back into the bag. Mounted his bike and started back home. Kannan continued the ride above the flyoverabove the railway tracks which carried the old black steam engines in which Amma, Akka and Kannan travelled during vacations when Appa was not to accompany them. The smell of the coal, the coal grit in the air, the smoke and the hoots were all replaced with modern engines and electric diesel hybrid engines of these days. But the mind could still show him those old pictures. The picture of Ammamma in her peacock blue saree at the railway station. The child in his was waving at his grandmother who was smiling for him. The ride back home was with a heavy heart but the pictures will make them lighter.

"Amma would be delighted to see those pictures," Kannan thought as he returned on his bike with a load of memories.

18

Prayers: As simple as it is

"Dear students. Happy Father'sDay to you and today we are proud to have one of our old students amidst us. Before I welcome him, I would like to take the opportunity to introduce him to you, though he is a man who needs no formal introduction," started the school head boy.

The school auditorium was full and students were eager to meet one of the well known speakers live for the next 40 minutes. Some were pulling each other's neck ties in fun, some seriously ready to take notes and some already feeling bored thinking about the talk. For Kannan it was yet another opportunity to share his thoughts with the generation to come. Some students assembled there were talking to each other about the videos they have seen on YouTube and about the way the speaker makes it really interesting.

"I have seen his videos. Have you?"

"Yeah, I have.I like him. Will he sign my autograph book?"

Kannan heard two boys behind him talk in hushed voice, while the head boy went on and on with the two-page introduction about the guest. There were cute boys; some with spectacles, some well-groomed, some really naughty, some with chubby cheeks and a cute little paunch, some by the looks revealed that they were the nerds of the lot. "Stu" as they are called, short for studious and the looks of those kids reminded Kannan about the same auditorium where he would stand along with his classmates for the morning school assembly. All his friends and the teachers came to his mind.

"... It's my honor and pleasure to welcome our school's old student and a successful creative director, known for his work, motivational speeches, inspiring millions, Mr. Kannan Iyer."

The hall reverberated with claps and Kannan's eyes shed a tear of joy. He walked up to the podium, gave a pat on the back of the school head boy, who seemed to be excited and eager to listen to Kannan speak. He rushed to his seat in the front row where the principal and some old teachers with some new, not known to Kannan were sitting.

"Dear students. Happy Father's Day to you all. It's really a proud moment for me," Kannan started without the usual four-folded paper which many carry with a written speech on it. "I have come a long way before I came here before you today and to speak to you. I owe what I am today to my Appa."

The naughty noise of the students subsided, and the voice was the only thing heard in the hall. And yes, the fans on the roof, which made the background score for Kannan's words.

"I don't want to bore you with a long speechbut want to ask you one question."

The kids who were taking notes from the first word Kannan spoke looked up and stopped scribbling on the notebooks.

"What do you want to be when you grow up?" asked Kannan and waited for an answer.

Kannan knew the obvious answer and there came a roaring mix of doctor, engineer, pilot and even actor and singer.

"Well, then let me ask you individually," he asked the students with a smile. Kannan was bending down to reach the microphone set to its maximum height, and still falling short of Kannan's expectation. He was bent over reaching the mic and with one hand on the podium folded like a news presenter and the other hand pointing to a smart young boy on the second row.

The young boy stood up and boldly started, "Sir... I want to be a science teacher."

"Ok," interrupted Kannan and asked the next boy.

"Sir, I want to be a pilot and make a lot of money so that we have a good life," was his reply.

"Interesting," said Kannan and pointed the next boy.

"Sir, I don't know. I just want to be like my dad when I grow up."

Kannan paused. He took a deep breath and asked the boy to sit down. Was that the answer he was looking for?

"Let me tell you about my father. My Appa is a simple man and once I asked him the same question," Kannan resumed from his silence. He saw his teachers look at him with the sense of accomplishment and happiness. As he narrated, his mind was being filled with that day when he was on vacation and the day started early owing to the jet lag.

Appa's day starts early in the morning when he gets up at 4 in the morning. He would slowly without making noise walk out of the bedroom and head to the pooja room. The lights of the pooja room would be turned on and he would stand there with folded hands. Kannan saw him praying silently with a sense of contentment on that day too. It was then he relished that Kannan was sitting there punching something on his smartphone and he smiled.

"You did not sleep?"

"No pa. Jet lag. I am fine. Shall I make coffee for you?"

He smiled again and said, "No. I will have to go for a walk now. Will have a tea there at the tea shop near the temple."

That was his usual morning routine: The walk, plucking flowers for pooja, a tea at the tea shop and humming some song to himself as he walks back home.

As he changed to his usual walking shirt and dhoti and came to the hall, where Kannan was sitting, he turned and asked.

"Do you want to come for a walk?"

Kannan smiled and said, "No, you enjoy your walk."

As Kannan finished the steaming hot filter coffee, which filled the room with the aroma, and the newspapers, Appa was back and he continued with his daily routine. The wash, the pooja, and then the visit to the nearby temple and back for breakfast. Kannan was intrigued by the never broken routine of Appa and while having the idlis with the special sambar which smelt of the masalas and coriander and would be enough to gobble down another dozen of idlis. He asked, "Appa," Kannan started the conversation while the devotional song was playing on the CD player, "Can I ask you something?"

Appa looked up and had another mouthful of the soft idlis, which Amma refers to as soft like jasmine idlis.

"What do you for pray at the temple?" Kannan asked.

"Nothing," was his reply.

"You mean you just go and pray.Pray for what?" Kannan was curious.

"Nothing. I don't say anything. I just get the pleasure in being there and ask nothing."

Kannan was spell bound for a second and again asked.

"You have asked for nothing all these 70 plus years?"

"Ah yes. Once. When I had given my exam for CA. I was finding it tough and prayed that I passed," Appa replied.

Kannan smiled and thought, "The greatness of my Appa is truly his simplicity."

Kannan narrated the incident to the students and continued his brief yet interesting speech at the school.

"God knows what is good for us and our prayers are heard. But do you really need to ask what you want when God knows what is best for you?"

The pin drop silence in the school auditorium was broken by a thunderous applause and continued so for a few minutes.

"Thank you and keep praying.Happy Father's Day," Kannan concluded, feeling choked, overwhelmed with the love he had for his Appa.

As he walked back to his seat in the front row, Kannan ran his fingers through his hair and without anyone seeing wiped the tear on the corner of his eye, smiled to himself thinking.

"We pray for so many things; silly or not.But I can never be simple as my Appa who achieved everything from being the best dad for his children, a role model for those at work and a friend to all, without ever asking anything for himself in prayers. But I pray for his health and happiness and I will keep doing it."

Kannan knew it was too much for the students or himself to follow but knew that there would be very few in this world who would be as simple as Appa, who would walk the world and make it difficult for others to believe.

But it was Father'sDay and Kannan remains proud to be the son to such a simple father, whose simplicity remains even today in Kannan's heart. Deep down in his heart, he wished that Appa was there to listen to the applause for him, but was sure that he would just smile and walk away.

19

The signature

Morning office time was busy as usual at the agency.

"Sir, signature please," said the office assistant.

Kannan was engrossed with a message on WhatsApp from Manoj.

Good work brother. Was nice meeting you.

The message had taken him back several years, not knowing that the office assistant was waiting with a blank expression on his face. Kannan drifted back to the school days. The morning school bell was a start to the new academic year. The assembly was special as everyone wore new uniforms and the air was filled with the smell of fresh new clothes. Every student was at his best for the first day at school after clearing the previous year of learning. The white shirts, red ties, with navy blue trousers and the smile on the face. The tie was crisp and did not have the ink from the previous years writing and learning. The belt was immaculate and the colors red and yellow remained so, which in due course would bleed to a dull orange mixed with the dirt of a year. The feeling in every student's heart was just one. A new year, new class, new things to learn or was it, back to the same company as the previous year, more time to have fun and boring classes again with new subjects and new teachers. Whatever be it, the freshness was like a bright newly blossomed garden.

The school band played the fanfare and the school flag hoisted. The excitement was in the air and prayers and national anthem ensued. Kids marched to their respective classes. Kannan ran to the band room in the basement to keep his trumpet back in the marked box and ran back to the class. The attendance was being taken and he interrupted.

"Sir. Please may I get in?"

The classes, the breaks and recess, evening prayer and the long bells. Days passed with monthly exams and first term exams were over. After holidays school started again. It was the day when the signed black school dairy had to be checked for signatures from their father as instructed by Varghese Sir. Class Prefect, Vinod, was on leave as he was down with fever. Kannan, being the vice prefect, started his official duty of checking the diaries. 62 students with a few missing, Kannan was fast enough to get the checking done before Varghese Sir would reach the class. He wrote down just three names and kept all the checked diaries on the teacher's table.

"Safeer, Bipin and Manoj," Varghese Sir called out the names and they stood up.

The class had the atmosphere of interrogation and inquiry. The usual noise which was cut by the three student's name who did not either sign their class diaries with the marks for the exam. Varghese Sir walked towards the last bench where Safeer with his loosely knotted tie was standing there with a wicked smile. He knew it was coming and was ready with the reply, "Sir tomorrow."

Varghese sir nodded and moved towards Bipin. He started crying and said, "Sir, me too ... tomorrow."

"Hmmm," said Varghese Sir and moved towards Manoj.

Manoj was standing there silent, when Kannan stood up and raised the complaint as if he was a public prosecutor in a court who raises the objection.

"Sir. His mother signed and not his father," Kannan said boldly.

"Why?" Varghese Sir asked Manoj looking stern.

Manoj stood there silent. Varghese Sir took the cane and tapped the desk strongly making it sound like a thunder for all the students.

"Sir. My father passed away when I was young."

The moment of silence had more to it. The teachers taking classes in the nearby classrooms could be heard. The open windows had sunlight falling into the class room. Kannan could not say anything. For him the day turned dark. The darkness made him shiver in his heart.

"Sit down," said Varghese sir and looked at Kannan.

The facts of life were being passed on to him that very moment and the looks of the class teacher seemed to ask him a thousand questions.

"Had I asked why. But what have I done?" thoughts hunted Kannan down. His smile faded away as if ink was washed from a paperin water. He had a heavy heart. The whole class moved on, but his heart remained at that moment.

"Can I give him a hug?" thought Kannan, but Manoj was nowhere around. That day was etched in his heart to this day.

"Sir, signature please," Kannan heard the office assistant impatiently waiting for his signature.

Kannan looked up mechanically. The smell of chalk dust and the books were gone. The bench and desks were not anywhere to be seen. The smell of packed lunch boxes, books and bags, the familiar smell of the classroom, the sounds of the cane and the teachers were all replaced by the hum of the air conditioner, the soft music being played in the in-house channel of the office and smells of a mix of perfumes. He travelled back to the present and quickly signed the paper.

"Give it to Ali," Kannan instructed and picked the phone again.

"Sorry," he typed on a message window then deleted it. And again typed "Sorry", and sent it to Manoj. It took Kannan more than two decades to say that one word, and kept the phone on the table.

Bzzzzzzzzzzzz ..... the phone vibrated and read "Incoming call ...Manoj".

Kannan picked the call and with no words to say he picked the call.

"Kanna. Did you send me a message saying sorry."

"Oh by mistake," Kannan said. His heart was as complex as many of us. Why is it difficult to apologize for a mistake. Why does it take long to make good for silly wrongs we did. Many questions still remains unanswered for Kannan like all others.

20

All in the family

"Kanna, come have this idly at least."

Amma was finding it hard to feed the four year old Kannan. He was excited and running all over seeing so many people gathered for the function in the evening. He would have a bite and run away and Amma had to hunt him down with the small plate of idlies, before giving him the next mouthful of idly with sugar and ghee, the way he liked it.

It was the anniversary function of the Lakshmi Hospital, which Kannan's paternal grandfather Late Mr. Kannan Iyer, the famous lawyer in the city, had built for his son, Kannan's Sambashivan Periyappa, Appa's elder brother. The hospital staff, relatives, friends and their family all were there for the evening function. Dr. Sambhashivan's house was more of a pent house atop the hospital building. It had nice gardens with flowers at its best, a tournament sized badminton court for all the kids to play and a home adjoining it where his family and his sister lived. It was the center of activity for the day as the open area was turned to be the arena of events as a part of the anniversary celebrations. From evening onward, all were busy decking up the place at its best. Chairs were arranged for seating the invitees, staff and relatives and there were many patients and bystanders who had come up to enjoy the festivities.

It was already getting late and Amma had to feed Kannan before he would get tired and doze off. Amma's world revolved around her two kids. Pachai was big enough to have her dinner, but Kannan - mothers know it better. Pachai was having fun with all the other cousins as usual and finished her dinner with them. The kitchen of Dr. Sambashivan's home was more of a catering centre for the evening. Crates of soda was piled up on one corner, huge drums of idli and vada was being moved out to the dining area for those who were already there having dinner. The smell of coriander in the sambar was enough for people to gobble away two idlis in one go. There were nurses and other staff who were getting ready for their part. The stage was dishing out programmes for those who wanted entertainment. The tableau which was the highlight of the evening had just finished, which had Krishna, Mohan's son as the patient, Dr. Parthasarathy as Hippocrates and Dr. Vasantha as his assistant as seen in the Hippocrates' famous painting. Amma rushed into the kitchen and took idlies to feed Kannan and was running since then behind him. The first idli took more than 15 minutes and it was the turn of the second.

The upcoming performance was a Kathakali dance recital and the artists were getting their makeup done. The face was painted and the beard, typical of Kathakali made of rice paste was being set for the main performer. He was lying on the mat on the ground and Kannan was standing and watching in amazement. Amma got a glimpse of Kannan standing there and rushed to him.

The green and the black with the white beard of rice paste, anyone would watch in amazement how it is done. The record for the thickest make up in the world belongs to this dance form of Kerala which remained a temple art and now commercialized as short capsules. The artists had to lie still for hours to get the makeup done. Kannan was looking at the red eyes of the artist being give the makeover looking at him.

"Kanna. Have one more piece. Please good boy," Kannan could hear Amma venting her helplessness.

"I am watching," said Kannan in his sweet voice with sugar all over his face and ghee smeared in the repeated attempts of feeding which failed.

The Kathakali artist smiled at him and Kannan was not so sure whether to smile back or not. Amma finally caught hold of Kannan's hand and pushed a piece of the sugar and ghee-soaked piece. Kannan kept looking at the makeup and the artist in amazement as he started chewing whatever had been just given to him, without even relishing the taste. It was a novel experience for him to see the preparations for Kathakali. The room had other artists getting their steel finger nails, red paint on the face, the ornaments for the dance, the long-starched cloth being tied round and round to make the umbrella like dress for another dancer. The music from the stage could be heard, it was a classical vocal recital being performed by Deepika, Mohan's daughter and Pachai, Kannan's Akka.

The artist, who was on the floor, said something to the person who was doing the makeup and he got up and brought a banana. He took it from the makeup artist and extended towards Kannan.

Kannan was scared and stepped back.

"Amma," Kannan shouted in amazement.

"Go take it," Amma told Kannan and thought to herself, that's an easy way to fill Kannan for the night.

Scared and surprised, Kannan slowly nudged towards the artist on the floor and took the banana from his hand and ran back to Amma and held on to her sari. Hugging her leg and hiding behind it. Amma took the banana from Kannan's hand, peeled it and gave it back to him.

"Eat quickly, see that man is looking at you, he would snatch the banana if you don't have it. Eat it quick, otherwise you would get stomach pain. That man is watching you eat." Amma's explanations and threats made Kannan eat the banana.

The mission to feed Kannan was accomplished and Amma took Kannan to the wash basin and washed his face and wiped his face with the edge of her sari. For a moment Kannan did not want to lose sight of what was happening around him and moved Amma's hand and sari to continue seeing the sights around him.

Amma took Kannan and went to the front row before the stage where Pachai was sitting with Appa. Sat down when the speakers gave out the Kathakali music and the performance started. The whole family sat there watching the performance reach its pinnacle and the curtains were down.

"That was an amazing Kathakali recital by Dr. Sambashivan and team." The announcement was loud and clear. The curtain went up once again when Sambashivan Periyappa, the man who was getting ready for the recital, the man on the floor who offered him the banana, came forward and smiled at Kannan. The young Kannan realized that the person whose performance he was adoring all this while was his Periyappa, and so did Amma realize the same. The shocked and shamed look on Amma's face for what all she said about him remained on the face for weeks.

It's all in the family.Dr Sambashivan had never asked Amma about the incident, but his smiles said it all.

21

Kannan's secret

Every time Venki Mama came home Kannan's happiness knew no bounds. When Amma got married, he was just 12 years old. There was a time when mother and daughter went to the labour at the same time, owing to the child marriage times of the past. Venki Mama was Venki to Kannan and more a brother than an uncle.

It was another summer vacation when Venki Mama had come home. He was a movie buff and his style varied according to the latest movies of Kamal Hassan or Mammootty. He was in college doing pre-egree, fourth group, and Kannan looked up to him knowing not what that was. He was a singer, did mimicry and was a handsome young man. His style had some influence on Kannan too. But there were times too, when Kannan and Akka had a tough time when he used to bully them, take Kannan's tricycle and ride sitting on top of it in which he would never fit in.

"Amma. Venki has taken my cycle again," Kannan would wail at the top of his voice.

Venki would smile when Amma would shout back from the kitchen, "Venki, they are kids. Leave them alone."

Probably Venki saw in Amma his mother too as they were very close to each other, more of inseparable brother and sister. Kannan much later even came to know that he hid under the bed when he accompanied Amma, when she had got married and come to their in-laws.

Kannan's eyes brighten up when Venki would direct plays for all the cousins to be staged before the family, when he would sing film songs with ease, when he would draw and paint. He too loved Kannan a lot. They would use the tape recorder to record stories from comics and create never heard before audio books in their own style. They would play the LP records and dance to the tunes. Akka was more of a studious type so they would enjoy all that with just the two of them.

"Paappa," as he used to call Amma as all others at home used to call her," I am going out for a movie to Mymoon Cinema."

"Here," Amma handed a few crumpled notes, which she saved from her daily shopping and hid in the rice box. Venki smiled and took the money happily.

"Amma I want to go to the cinema too," Kannan rushed and hugged Amma's legs tightly as a plea.

Venki, to avoid taking him said quickly, "It's a horror movie. You will get scared, I will take you tomorrow to Kamal's movie."

Kannan started crying and was pacified by Amma with a sweet laddoo from the lot Venki had brought from Ammamma. He walked away with a tough face towards

Venki, but it still looked cute. A five year old naughtily trying to say with looks that he won't share the laddoo.

Venki rushed to the theatre. The white boards had black bold letters. Mymoon in orange letter had the name *Varumayin Niram Sivappu.*

He turned and saw the huge yellow hued poster with Kamal on it, giving a feeling that the hero looking towards him. Huge larger than life cut out of Kamal Hassan waving his hand with red plastic flower garlands on them. Venki transformed to Venki Hassan and adjusted his hair and scanty beard started walking in a style which he thought was the way Kamal would, and thought to himself.

"What if someone thinks that I am Kamal Hassan," the obvious thoughts many had looking at the poster.

He saw the queue for the Dress Circle at the cinema and thought to himself,"I have enough cash for Balcony and Mymoon has a beautiful one. Should enjoy this day."

He walked up to counter where there were a few people. He looked around and saw young girls, old uncles and many others around him. Being Venki Hassan now, he tried to look away in style at the same time glance the girls. In fact, a few of them were looking at him. He rubbed his beard a bit as Kamal would. His happiness knew no bounds, Kamal movie, Balcony, at the newly inaugurated Mymoon theatre, girls looking at him... what more to ask for.

In style he walked into the theatre and the movie started. In the dark he kept looking if someone else was looking at him thinking that Kamal was watching the movie with them. In fact, he was watching the movie for the third time. But this time it was special, alone in style. An hour and a half of the movie passed quickly. Intermission - the huge screen read. He got up retaining the airs around him. He walked out of the hall towards the cafeteria singing.

Sippi irukkuthu muththum irukkuthu kavitha paada neram illadi rasathi ..., the song which played in the movie and Kamal Hassan was at his best in it.

He moved into the whole lot of people stretching their arms towards the person serving coffee and bought a cup of coffee. He got his cup and carefully moved away towards the display wall with a whole lot of vertical glass strips. He looked at it and saw over a dozen of images of himself. He had a naughty smile seeing it and put his hand into the right pocket of his bell bottom pants, which was in vogue then. He had hid a pack of Charminar cigarette pack from the world, his personal secret. Took one and lit a match in style. He took a puff and looked at the mirrors to see over a dozen of images of the hero in him again and again. He took a puff and blew it out with his head tilted carelessly. He looked at those images and ... and.... Venki's heart sank. There appeared over a dozen images of Mohan Mama, his sister's brother in law, behind him. The world seemed to melt inside him.

"He saw me smoke. He would go and tell Paappa. Oh no..."

He thought no more. The Kamal Hassan in him vanished. He was Venki again, caught red handed with a cigarette in it. He ran downstairs through the stairs in amazing speed. He would have a promise for India in the Olympics then. His eyes were red and tears started rolling. He ran home in the same speed. Amma was preparing dinner. Kannan was playing as usual with his toy gun on the sofa. Venki was panting, trying to get a breath.

"The movie is over?" queried Amma.

"Paappa ..." Venki got a breath and replied, sweating profusely. "Come," and grabbed Amma's hands and went into the kitchen.

Appa was in the hall checking his account sheets from office. That grabbed Kannan's attention and he held his gun in hand and swiftly moved behind the kitchen door to know what the matter was.

Still breathing hard Venki confessed to Amma.

"Paappa, Mohan Mama saw me smoke. Don't say anything. I will not do it again. Please."

His tone was apologetic and wanted an assurance that Thatha doesn't know about it, which Amma would eventually do. Kannan had a smile on his face. He got something to keep Venki from taking his tricycle - maybe get him to do what he wants - a secret. Kannan went back to the sofa with a smile, waiting for the opportunity to use his newly got secret. Moments of achievement.

22

The one day master chefs

"Kanna, you cut the onions," Akka took the charge of the kitchen and instructed how the onions should be sliced.

Appa and Amma had gone for a wedding to Coimbatore and the house was left to the kids for two days. Akka being the elder one took charge and dinner was the point of contention. The plan was to make something light for dinner. The discussion finally culminated on making bread upma. Akka started with a smile, a person who rarely entered the kitchen when Amma was at work and she was feeding Akka before she had to rush to the school. The bookworm of sorts, the only three things she loved were text books, notes and sleep. Tall fair and tender as a climber, her name Pachai – green - was apt. She could also be dubbed Charulatha, the tender branch of a sapling. Her big spectacles, twin braided long hair, fair skin, bright eyes like Appa and silent disposition she looked more like a doctor even when she was at school. She was 17 and Kannan was 14. Not kids anymore, but to parents they are always kids. The teen team ransacked the kitchen to gather all they needed to make bread upma. Kannan was confident that a girl of her age would know what to do. Systematic Akka made the checklist and Kannan was the assistant to the sous chef of the day at home.

Bread, onion, tomato, ginger, turmeric powder, sambar powder, ghee, salt, oil, mustard seeds, fresh green chilles and a few curry leaves from the plant in the backyard.

"Long or small pieces?" Kannan checked with Akka.

"Anyway you like. Just the two of us. No decorations needed, but I would prefer it long," replied Akka seriously thinking about the procedure ahead - cooking.

Tears rolled down Kannan's eyes, not of sorrow or happiness, but from the onions. The acrid onions were nicely cut and chilies washed and cut too. Kannan started with the ginger and tomatoes.

She cut the bread into squares meticulously as if she had a lab exam of dissecting the bread pieces. Put the kadai on the gas cook top and poured the ghee. She put the sliced bread and started mixing it.

"Pachai," Kannan shouted mockingly, "If you are frying the bread, better have the burner on."

Though Akka did not like the comment and seemed another fight was imminent between the siblings, she smiled and lit the gas stove. The bread turning golden brown in the kadai and the kitchen filled with the smell of ghee and fried bread. Kannan was getting hungry and the aroma fired the passion in his stomach - to eat. Akka switched the gas off and waited thinking what to do next.

It was for the first time, Amma had left them alone and every time they were alone, they would start a fight. Amma was worried but had to attend the wedding. Clear instructions were given to Akka about what needs to be done and what not. Kannan was told just one thing.

"Be a good boy and take care of Akka."

Akka, like a master chef, poured oil into the pan and added the mustard seeds. She was not used to the splutter and it was very obvious with how she moved away and stood as if she had lit a fire cracker waiting to go off. Kannan looked up and gave her the onions, ginger, green chilies and curry leaves. All were added and the cooking lab came to life. The onions sweat to a transparent white and the smell was heavenly or was it because of the hunger which had struck both of them.

Then the red chopped tomatoes were added for color, a pinch turmeric powder, a spoonful of sambar powder, a little salt. The cooking would yield them their dinner, or that was the intention. Tomatoes lost all hope and got squished in the heat. Everything seemed to be going nice. The bread pieces were added and tossing started. Akka kept looking at Kannan and the kadai and Kannan did vice versa. The fruits of their efforts. The smiles on their face was at the crescendo.

"Akka knew how to make bread upma," Kannan thought.

That was when Akka remembered the procedure to make rava upma - water for cooking. And she poured enough water to sink all their efforts into the pan. The water made the dish look like a colored paste. Everything turned to be a blob. As the say in Hindi, *kiye karaye pe paani phir gaya*. The ghastly looks on their face was worth an Oscar. The bubbles on the blob made it look like some pink paste that was being incinerated in a cauldron by the witches; sticky and viscous. The silence crept in, the dreams of dinner slowly started vanishing. What to do?

Akka put in all her strength to heat the water out of the dish that would have been dinner tonight. The pan started moving with the ladle as the paste was getting thicker.

"All in vain," the same thought filled the young minds.

Probably the symbolism of the light bulb above a person's head for a bright new idea was understood by Pachai that day. The bulb did glow with a new idea. She quickly took the container with gram flour, added some salt and chili powder and poured the villain - water and mixed it to a fine paste. She took the cool paste and made it into balls, dipped it in the gram flour paste and dropped it into the hot oil in a frying pan which she had set by then. Kannan did not have a clue what was happening. But lo and behold, a new dish was born.

"Pachai, what do we call this?" Kannan asked trying to eat one fried new dish by the master chef.

"Blajji," Akka smiled and christened it.

Tasted good but the looks did not matter. The plate full of Blajji were taken to the dining table with respect and kitchen lights were switched off, with no intention to return in the near future. Later Blajji was a dish to remember for both of them. However good or bad a dish looks, hunger makes it taste so good. A new lesson learnt.

23

Faith forever

Heated discussions were always intriguing for Kannan throughout his life, whether he was a part or not. Many of his thoughts, actions and decisions were born out of such discussions. It is during the teens when everyone had the urge to leave the blood boil and think to rebel against anything conventional. Kannan had strong belief in God and was so devout, that he would spend hours praying even at a tender age of five. He had his own set of idols and considered them more sacred than anything in the world. The young mind of five was influenced by many instances which made him more and more intense in his prayers. The prayer time was when he used to talk to his Gods in person. Ask them what they wanted, tell them about school and friends and everything that happened to him on a day to day basis.

"Would he take a path of an ascetic?" Amma thought seeing all this and shared the worry with Appa, who was alarmed but kept his cool.

He was put to drawing and painting, which was his other passion other than prayers, as that could take him away from the path Appa and Amma worried he would take. But even when he lived his passion of being in the world of colors, the faith in him was going strong. He had his own time with God in private for hours still. It was also the outcome of how he was treated by his cousins who kept him away from all the fun they had as he was too small.

The cousins together had a game of 'City City' where each one would have a part to play more like a live arcade game or Farmville. Deepika, Mohan Mama's daughter, would run a mock restaurant 'Rock View Restaurant' on the pile of stones on one corner with dosa made of paper being served in small aluminum plates. Pachai would become the vegetable dealer with all that she could gather from the area - like the small garden huckleberries (*Manathakkali* as they call it), ripe guavas and jamun from the tree in front of Mohan Mama's house or even tamarind from the nearby trees. They had their own currency and Krishna and Ram, the elder ones would take their cycles and be the public transport. The city even had police and Raj would be the one with his cute police uniform with a whistle on dangling in a rope nicely tucked in the top left pocket of the shirt.

"You are God's child and you should run the temple," said the elder ones to Kannan.

He would wait for someone to come to the temple where he would have an orange colored Hanuman fridge magnet as the deity. But everyone would be busy in their work.

"Please come to the temple for darshan or aarti," Kannan would plead to the others.

"Don't come out of the temple, be there," would be the reply.

The game would go on till dusk, where they would have successfully avoided the menace of handling the young Kannan. He would keep on talking to God with his bright big eyes filled with tears.

"Why don't they let me play? Please Hanuman... Please Maruti...," he would plead.

But this was a daily affair and he was taken closer to Gods who would listen to him without rebuke. He moved into his own world of prayers and colors. He felt safe being alone than being avoided by the others. Had that made him more secluded and remorse or is it the faith that was built through the stories of Gods and Goddesses he heard.

Every moment of his life was spent in thoughts of Gods and prayers. He was stuck on to it for a very long time till one day. He was walking by the side of the old tiled house of Mohan Mama. He was pulled by a heated argument. It was a discussion between Murugan Anna and Mohan Mama. Murugan Anna was doing his Engineeringbut had his mind in magic. He had a green trunk filled with magic items and he would perform from time to time. The twelve year old Kannan looked up to him and thought he would be a great magician one day. His thoughts were different and were considered rebellious.

"Mohan Mama. I don't agree with your thought," he said and Kannan thought, how anyone can talk like that to Mohan Mama.

It was a discussion between the past and the present, a dialogue between generations. Murugan was in his carelessly folded full sleeve white shirt and khakis and Mohan Mama was in the tradition dhoti and shirt with his forehead smeared with holy ash and sandal paste. Murugan was fair and turned red while talking to Mohan Mama who kept his calm silent nature and would speak in a very low tone.

"These temples and your beliefs all are false," Kannan was shattered to hear it from Murugan, someone who was his idol.

For a second he thought, "Is it true, Gods, temples...," He was more fascinated by the thought.

"You put money in the temple and ask for what you want. You pay money as offering for something in return. Is that not bribe?" Murugan asked in a raised voice to one of the respected personalities of the family, Mohan Mama.

"These are Communist thoughts and we don't think like that in our family. You are misled," said Mohan Mama.

But that was an answer not very satisfying for Kannan or Murugan, though he was not in the discussion. The discussion moved into rational thoughts and things which Kannan had never heard before. He could see Mohan Mama fuming in anger when his sister's son was speaking a language no one spoke in the very orthodox family. The words like culture, tradition and higher spirituality was being thrown on Murugan, which was dealt with thoughts of Voltaire, Engels and other rational thinkers with facts and figures. The discussion ended with a decision that Murugans thoughts have been poisoned by bad influence.

It was a turning point in Kannan's life too. He thoughts started moving astray and with no one to guide him. His choice of books moved from classics and mythology to Engels, Rousseau and more on rational thoughts. After moving to Trivandrum, Kannan's loneliness and thoughts made him difficult to manage for Amma alone. They got him a tutor, a college student, who would make him sit in one place and study. Tutored by a Suresh, an ardent Communist Marxist Leninist doctrine follower, Kannan was moving more towards atheism and rationalism. Their study time turned to be study classes for extreme Communism. From

Cuba to Chile and China to Russia. More than tutor and student, they became comrades discussing revolution and rationalism. He stopped prayers and spent very less time in them. He moved towards the world of letter and books, still alone. The loneliness built a world of his own within himself.

Kannan's faith was replaced by red thoughts. He remained between being agnostic or atheist till his time in Dubai in 1998. He had left his job and was about to return. With not much money left with him even to buy a square meal, the scorching summer sun, and the thoughts of why all this had to happen was dragging him into more thoughts. All he had were a few friends. The bearded, cafeteria shawarma maker Ismailikka, Feroz, the waiter there, Javed at the restaurant on his way back, Parvez and a few other. He had nothing to tell them, nothing to give them. Kannan was leaving for good and had no idea what his next moment would be. His thoughts were as dry as his throat cracking for a drop of water. He wished he had a coin to pick up a bottle of cold water from the vending machine.

"Is there God? Why is it that I have to go through all this?" Kannan wondered.

He was walking by the wayside when his thoughts were disrupted by a call from behind.

"Iyer ... Iyer..." Javed called out at the top of his voice.

He would meet Javed on the late evening walks from office to the apartment every day. Javed and his friends worked for a small restaurant and they had not been getting their salaries for months. The chacha who used to make rotis in the restaurant used to give him rotis at times.

Javed, with his red waiters vest and black pants, came running and took a bunch of soiled notes and placed it in Kannan's hands, a few hundred dirhams in total.

"We would have done the same if our brother was stranded here. Keep this. You will need it." Javed's eyes had tears of joy and Kannan's heart filled with tears which were looking for an outlet through the eyes. Kannan never new whether he would be able to repay them for the love they showered on him then. He looked up to the sky with a scorching sun or was it his mind where he felt the heat but the wind of love cooled him in an instant.

A moment can change your life for sure and this one did change Kannan's life. God's works in ways we can never decipher. The touch on the shoulder from Javed was God's hands for sure. Kannan never doubted his faith from then on. Every breath was more of a prayer since then, even today.

24

The last moments ...

After years of service in the Harijan Welfare department, Sivaswami Iyer, a respected government official, devout father and Thatha as Kannan called him, retired from official duty. His life and family could only move on, only if he had a job to pursue as his sons were yet to secure a job and one was still in school and his daughter, Lakshmi got married just four years back. His life revolved around his home, temple and his work.

A six foot tall, strong man with silver white hair colored black with the trutone stick, always wearing his preferred snuff brown colored shirt and dhoti, with the holy ash smeared on his forehead, his charisma is something which can never be described with mere words. He stood tall undaunted even when he had to work as an account in an electronics shop at the ripe age of 61. The man who loved Sheaffers and Waterman pens but could never afford it. His earning barely could make both ends meet, but the smile never left his face, the hope which his prayers gave him made him strive with a smile. His happiness knew no bounds with the birth of Lakshmi's daughter, Pachai, the first daughter in the next generation. His treasure was enriched by the birth of Kannan after three years. Every time they came home for vacations, Sivaswami would stretch himself to the limits to give them the best he could.

Kannan always remembered the stories, the way he prayed morning and night, the trips they use to go together, the temple visits, the journey to the beach in the double decker, his workplace, his humility. He was a living text book to Kannan in all ways.

"*Muththucharam, thangakudam*," he meant every letter in those words as he considered Akka and Kannan the treasures of his life, the pearl necklace and the golden pot.

Every night was story time for Kannan and Akka by the side of the cane easy chair in the verandah of the twin house. By late evening, tired from work Thatha would come home with special treats for his treasures. Sweets, pakoras, mangoes or whatever he could get with the little money he spared for the special time of the year in his wooden safe box. He looked forward to that time of the year when they would be home.

When his four sons, and Kannan's family would be having dinner, Thatha would finish his wash and be sitting in front of the pictures of Gods in a white dhoti, with a silver lamp glowing in its divine brightness. He was fair and the color of the holy white ash could barely be seen different in his forehead or chest. He would be chanting the Lalithasahasranamam with a pinch of holy ash held tight between his fingers of the right hand. Having finished his prayers he would go to the kitchen and find hardly anything to have for dinner. He would have a glass of buttermilk and consider it dinner with the happiness of having fed everyone in the house. He would then walk across the road to get his regular betel nuts, leaves and relish the pan to its fullest. For Kannan and Akka that was an interesting sight to watch when he would chew green leaves and make his tongue turn red.

After the pan, was the time for the favorite stories of Sahasramallan the thief, Ekabudhdhi the frog, the lion who married the girl, and many many stories. His stories were accompanied by the smell of the flowers in the courtyard, the smell of betel leaves and fruits specially bought for his dear ones. Stories would end with both of them yelling, "Thatha ... one more story ... one more story ...," and the tell a tale would continue till late.

Kannan's last memories of Thatha was when he had arrived at the railway station while Appa, Amma, Kannan and Akka were on their way to Bombay for a vacation. Amidst the hustle and bustle of the railway station, Kannan saw Thatha in his regular brown shirt and dhoti with a watermelon in his hand. The ten year old Kannan's eyes sparkled. Thatha gave Amma the watermelon and said, "Lakshmi, kids will love this. It is very sweet. Take care of them."

They reached Bombay after three days. They booked for all the trips and sightseeing and returned to the room in BARC Quarters in Trombay. The next morning was fun filled for Kannan and Akka. They went on clicking pictures and getting excited about the new place and the sights.

The same morning back home Thatha was not feeling well. He called Venki and Padmanabhan his two sons and wished to go to see a doctor as he was feeling uncomfortable.

"Should be gas trouble," said Padhu and by then Venki went to the taxi stand to get the taxi.

Three of them got ready and Thatha opened his wooden safe box and took some cash and put it in his pocket. He pinned his black pen in the shirt and wore his bakelite shell frame glasses on. They were about to reach the hospital and Thatha smiled at Padhu. Put his hand into his shirt pocket and handed the money to him.

"You will need the money."

He kept his hand on the shoulder of Venki and smiled.

It was afternoon and Appa had upset his stomach owing to the change in food or water. They decided to rush back to the room. Kannan and Appa went first. Kannan as usual opened the door. There were two chits on the floor when the door opened. Kannan picked the chits when Appa was rushing in. He read out slowly as much as he could gather.

"URGENT MESSAGE. To Mr. Gopal. Father-in-law expired."

Kannan understood nothing but seeing Appa's eyes turn red and him standing still, gave him the gravity of the situation. He would hear no more stories from his beloved grandfather. He would see him no more. Kannan still remembers his Thatha as the man who would hold his hands tight at the beach when getting to feel the waves on his legs. The man with a red tongue telling him all the dear stories. The man who got him the sweetest of possible ways in the best way he could. Life moves on, but we tend to stop at certain junctures. By the time they reached Thatha had been cremated, leaving a void, never to have seen his still motionless body. His stories and chant are the treasures for Kannan and Akka to this date.

25

December will never be the same again

The month of December was very special to Kannan. Not just because it was the month of Christmas and holidays. Somehow many incidents were destined to happen in that month. It being the holy month of Christmas where he would be more of a Santa Claus to many with gifts and help from his side, as much as he could. It was on the 8th of the month, when he got married against the wish of Appa and Amma. It was the month which gave him shivers when he heard the train in which Amma was coming from Palakkad had a bomb blast. Though Amma survived the accident, the date December 6th was not so happy for Kannan, so wasn't it for many Indians for obvious reasons. There were many happy memories associated with that month too, but the one sad day, which was written with an indelible ink in his book of life was the day, December 17th.

He had just turned 16 that October. The morning of 17th Appa and Amma were hurrying and looked very sad and shocked. Amma was in tears, she had come home from the hospital very late the previous night. Amma was in tears and her eyes were red. Appa was gravely silent. Kannan woke up to this and saw Akka also crying. The facts of life were not still engraved in the soft stone tablet, the young mind of Kannan.

Amma walked into Kannan's room and she was incessantly crying. Kannan could not bear the sight as he never wanted to see her cry. He had seen her cry when his Thatha, her father passed away and by the time they reached from Bombay, he had already been cremated. The thought choked Kannan. It's Ammamma; his mentor, friend, philosopher, singer, his grandmother. Will he not see her again?

"Kanna ...Ammamma ...," she said and broke into more tears.

Kannan was shocked and could not fathom the pain he felt in his heart. His thoughts drifted back in time.

The old kitchen where Ammamma was making something special for them, as they reached the previous evening for the annual vacations.

"Nataraja.... grind it more finely," Ammamma said in a loud voice standing near the firewood stove with the huge black cauldron of oil.

Kannan was standing and watching in awe, straight from bed, awakened by the smell of frying and the sweet smell of sugar being made to a syrup. The way she poured the finely ground paste in a cloth piece and deftly fried jilebies on the hot oil.

"Kanna," she fondly called and handed him a hot jilebi just lifted from the sugar syrup in the tray nearby by on the table with a blue self patterned rexine sheet snugly nailed.

Kannan gobbled up the jilebi in no time and that was his first lesson in cooking. She had taught Akka and Kannan crochet, knitting, embroidery and all that she knew. Her swift hands made it look so easy then. Kannan came back to the present and saw Appa getting things packed. His mind drifted again.

Paahimaam sree rajarajeswari ..., the song lingered in his mind.

Ammamma used to sing so many songs for Akka and him. The songs and the sweetness of the burfies, the jilebies, the sambar and idlis she made, the taste of the coffee, the curries all came to his mind again. The movies she used to love and the love she had in her eyes - all were images flashing in Kannan's mind. The way she used to fondly fight with Thatha, the six foot fair and handsome man even at 60, who smelled of *bhasmam* (holy ash with the smell of roses) and sandal all the time. His snuff colored shirt and the red silk saree, the diamond studded peacock nose pin, the white swan necklace, the jasmine flowers on her braided and put up hair and the gold bangles Ammamma used to wear. Images were flashing as if someone had played video in rewind mode.

It was a cool December morning and Kannan was playing in front of the house when he saw Damodaran's cycle rickshaw. He saw from a distance Damodaran smoke the beedi in his usual style and kicked the pedals of the green flapped rickshaw was the one which used to take Kannan to his drawing classes. He saw Ammamma in it and was so delighted. He never understood why at that age as to why she had to be walked into the house with help. Her bag and a huge drum of burfee as usual were there. Kannan grabbed the burfee tin and walked along with Damodaran who helped her get down and walk with great difficulty. He saw Ammamma's hand bent and not moving.

"250. High sugar," Kannan heard Amma tell Appa sadly.

"Paralysis."

He felt he was in some spelling bee competition where he wished to ask for the meaning. He understood she won't be able to make yummy jilebis like before. Her eye sight was failing due to the condition and that she was under treatment.

Then for many years he had seen the vibrant grandmother who used to deck up even for a movie she used to go turn to someone who could not see or move without help. She would talk to them about songs, cooking, art, craft, temples and even when in bed, she used to instruct the cooks in such a way that the dishes had the same taste as she used to make or at least near it. She could no longer enjoy the sweets, nor enjoy the coffee with sugar. Kannan and Akka used to watch her drink the bitter gourd juice which was supposed to be having medicinal values and the bitterness used to give her loose stomach convulsions. They used to keep watching the stomach move and laugh. Those laughs made her forget the bitterness and vacations were days when they enjoyed these sights and Thatha's stories.

Thatha had gone and now Ammamma. Kannan cried but was numb. Life ends for everyone. The lesson was being engraved in the mind by God himself. Losses. May be time will lessen the pain, but the mind will never erase those memories.

"Kanna," he heard the musical voice call him, but in his mind. A mother of five, who lived her life in style enjoying till the moment 'sugar' took the sweetness away from her life and then lived with the memories of those days, all which will now remain memories. Those were the thoughts when Kannan reached the hospital where everyone was silent or crying. A few were talking about the last moments of her life and Ammamma's body lay still in bed.

Decembers for Kannan will never be the same again. Years later, whenever Kannan sang, or made sweets or watched movies, or even smiled he could hear Ammamma's voice call him again and again.

"Kanna ...."

26

Story tellers are born

A few words go a long way in life. Jeffrey Archer's interview on radio was playing on Kannan's car, loud and clear. The monotony of the daily commute to the office was broken by the only companion radio. Questions and answers about his books, scam, politics and the most desired question from the interviewer grabbed Kannan's attention.

"What would you suggest people who want to be writers?"

Quick was the reply from Jeffrey, "Story tellers are born."

There was a brief silence and it meant a lot. It was a blow to the question and Kannan's indelible marker in the mind wrote it down in the mind forever. He was reminded of the story with vivid explanations and expressions given to it by Thatha.

The smell of the night, the flowers, the familiar smell of holy ash and the freshness of the soap, Thatha chewing his pan, his dhoti after his prayers, all rushed to Kannan's mind. He became the same kid who sat next to the easy chair where Thatha sat chewing the betel leaves and started. (The story has many lines in Tamizh and the translations are in the parenthesis. The language is retained to keep the authenticity and the way it is told.)

"Once there was a man who never wanted to work. He was married and his wife was sick and tired of the laziness of her husband. She shouted at him...," and Thatha's eyes had all the expressions for Kannan and Akka to see the character in the story well in his face.

"Don't you feel like taking care of the family? Won't you earn a single penny?" Thatha narrated wiping a drop of the red spit from the pan he was chewing with a hand towel he had covered his shoulder.

"Dum dum dum," he continued, "And the person from the palace was announcing....," he changed his voice like the announcement from the court of the kind.

"Lend me your ears of lover of letters, the Royal court of Raja Raja Chozhan hereby announce a sum of 1000 gold coins for the best poem about his majesty Raja Raja Chozan, the lover of letters."

Hearing this Kannan and Pachai opened their eyes wide with hands on their cheeks with amazement.

"Hey you *mannunnimaappilayae* (lazy bones). Listen. At least write something and get the prize money", the wife shouted and threw a pot at her husband," said Thatha. Kannan chuckled along with Pachai.

Thatha continued with the story, "... and he set out with packed lunch of thaiyir saadam (curd rice) and pickles. He walked to a nearby temple and sat in the shade. He started to try and write a few lines and wrote the first thing that came to his mind *mannunni maappilayae* (Lazy bones) and looked up the tree and saw a crow and wrote *kaakrirae* (You sound like a crow), then he turned to see a nightingale sing and wrote *kookirayae* (You hoot like a bird). And he was hungry and ate the whole lunch," Thatha said patting his stomach as if he had had the lunch. "The food made him tired and he slept off and was woken up by a huge rodent which ran by him from the temple. He got irritated and wrote down in his poem as *ungappan kovil peruchaazhi* (Your father is the temple rodent). The poor lazy bones looked for more and more inspiration to find nothing. Finally, by dusk he had reached the palace and he wrote the closing which came to his mind *kana pinna thenna manna chozhanga perumaane* (Random words with a salutation as a closing to the king).

Kannan was on the verge of an excitement outbreak though he would have heard the same story many times. He asked, "and then ... Thathta." Pachai gave a nasty look to Kannan and ask him to sit silent and listen to the story.

"And where were we," asked Thatha and recollecting the point where Kannan had interrupted and continued.

"So the poem was ready and it read,"

"Mannunni maappilayae,
Kaakiraye kookiraye,
Ungappan kovil peruchaazhi,
Kanna pinna thenna manna,
Chozhanga perumaane."

Thatha took another betel leaf and slowly applied the white chuna on it and chewed it with a few pieces of broken betel nut before he went on with the story,"And he went and submitted the poem to the king. He was the last to reach and the piece of leaf in which he had scribbled the lines reached the minister. The minister had to read it out and was scared as he could lose his head for reading out this poem, but he had to read it aloud. And the minster said, "Amazing

amazing ... best possible ... simply divine ... oh what lines ... superb"" Kannan and Pachai saw Thatha transform himself as the minister who announced it.

Thatha smiled and looked at the excitement of his dear grandchildren and went on, "The king wanted to know what the lines where and the minister started."

"What was the first line?" asked Thatha.

"*Mannunni maappilaye* ...," Kannan shouted with excitement.

Thatha leaned forward to Kannan and Pachai and said, "The minister said, "what an opening the son in law who eats mud".The son in law of the Lord himself, Lord Krishna, who ate mud in his childhood. Amazing amazing.*Kaakiraye* - you protect the world, *kookiraye*- you are the ruler of the world. *Ungappan* (Your father) *ko* (World's) *vil* (Bows) *peru*(Big) *chaazhi* (Lion) - means your father is a great warrior who was a lion in archery. When the minster stopped, the King Raja Raja Chozhan asked, "Wonderful. What's the last line"? To which the minister replied.

"*Kanna pinna thenna manna chozhanga perumane,*" was the turn of Pachai who could not hold back the excitement.

"Hmmmm," Thatha said, "*Kannanukku pin thennattukku mannanaakiya chozhanga perumaane* (The only apt ruler for the southern land after Lord Krishna is you your Majesty) and the King was so happy to make him the courts poet and gift him the promised 1000 gold coins.And he lived happily ever after," thus ending the story, Thatha hugged Kannan and Pachai saying, "*Muththu charam, thanga kudam,*" and took them to bed.

The story was so vivid that Kannan tries, even now, when he gets a chance to be with kids, to tell the story how Thatha had told him. But as Jeffrey said, Thatha was a story teller and Kannan could never match him in anyway. As he drove away from the traffic, Kannan had those last lines in his lips *Kanna pinna thenna manna chozhanga perumaane* and repeated them like the young Kannan used to dance and say those lines and smiled.

27

Pain, left over

The counseling room was neat and tidy but those who walked into the room had made a mess out of their minds. Kannan had been practicing in the hospital for a few years now. At the age of 45, he was already looking 60. Like the winds in the desert leaves the dunes with ripples, the wrinkles on the face of Kannan spoke volumes about his life. Tied long hair, salt and pepper beard with a red pull over he would look like Santa Claus. The white coat for doctors was just a cover to the over-sized counselor dressed in black shirt and dark blue denims. The door outside had the white board - Kannan Iyer, Clinical Psychologist. The white tissue covered bed was not meant for most of the patients who walk into his room, and so the sheets were white as it had been laid. The table had a few books, a *Diagnostic Manual DSM V,* and a writing pad and a pen. Kannan was on a call when the nurse walked in.

"Sir," the nurse interrupted.

Kannan pushed his spectacles up the bridge of his long nose and looked towards her as if to ask what it was.

"Bala is back with his daughter," she replied.

"I will call back," said Kannan over the phone and gestured the nurse to send them in.

Bala, a man of around 35, well-dressed with uncombed hair and shabby beard, sunken eyes tired from crying walked in. He took his seat and asked his daughter to sit, with gestures. The room was very silent. Strangely it did not look as if the child was in the room. Kannan looked at her and asked.

"So how is my sweetheart?"

She nodded with a smile. With her well-braided hair, bright brown eyes, smooth baby skin shining, faded blue denim jacket and the jeans, the cute 7 year old said nothing but nodded and smiled.

"Will she talk to me doc?" Bala asked and could not hold his tears back.

Kannan buzzed the attendant and a young lady in white uniform walked in.

"Take Henna to the play area," he said.

As the attendant took Henna out of the room, Kannan turned his attention towards Bala.

"Henna could not bear the loss and she has lost her mother Bala.You know adults can't handle losses. She is a kid. But let me refer you to Dr. Sreekumar. He will do the needful. It is temporary. She is in shock and will be alright," assured Kannan and quickly wrote a referral note on the pad and handed it over to Bala, who took it and walked out of the room.

"The mind is so misunderstood, yet no one minds it," thought Kannan to himself. Bala and Henna were the last to visit him on the late Wednesday afternoon. Kannan reclined on the chair and on the intercom checked for anymore patients. The answer that he was free for the evening reeled Kannan into the past.

With closed eyes he could still remember the room where his uncle Natarajan was admitted. The dimly lit, enough wide corridors, of Lakshmi Nursing Home with rooms on either side with ailments of all kinds. The corridors smelled of Dettol and had a few cleaning it over and over again leaving the moist smell to penetrate the nose, leaving it numb for a while. The night fall made the whole hospital sleepy and silent. Kannan was a boy of 7 when Natarajan Mama was admitted for an appendicitis operation. He knew nothing about the procedure, but that his Mama was not well and operation would be done on him. As they say in kiddish language, his Mama had *uvvavu*.

Kannan walked into the room with Amma, to see the dense and curly black-haired Natarajan mama with a thick moustache like a brush, in bed and trying to sit up. He was wearing the green uniform given to him by the hospital. It looked funny enough for Kannan to see his uncle in a lady like dress.

"So the procedure is tomorrow," Amma said, for which he nodded with a smile.

Kannan was in his own world and sketching something on his small sketch book. Amma and Natarajan Mama were talking about a whole lot of things, when their attention was broken by a knock on the door.

"Have to give him an injection," said the nurse in a stern voice.

The sight of the needle made Kannan and Natarajan Mama equally nervous. After the scare bout was over and the nurse stepped out, Kannan saw a girl standing at the door.

"Can I come in?" she asked

She was in her teens for sure. Dark complexioned, with a brown long blouse and a green long skirt, big eyes like a white saucer holding a black ball, and loosely tied hair with oil on it. She walked in and asked:

"Uncle. You are afraid of needles, right?"

Natarajan Mama laughed. She wished Amma and lightly patted on Kannan's face. Sat down on the bystander cot in the room. She was smiling for sure but had a strange sadness on her face.

"This is Keerthana. She is in the next room," said Natarajan Mama to Amma.

She went on talking to both of them as if she had known them for years. About her house, about her school, her friends, her likes, dislikes and a whole lot. She stopped for a moment and asked.

"Can I sing a song for you?In Sreeragam, classical?"

Natarajan Mama, who used to play the Mrudangam professionally, showed his interest and accepted the offer from the girl. They were all ears. Kannan's eyes shined as he loved music too.

"Akka sings. She sings Sreeragam well," he broke in with his comment.

For which Keerthana smiled and started singing, *Karuna cheyvaan enthu thaamasam Krishna* .... And as soon as she started singing the whole corridor was filled with melodious voice and filled it with a unique ambiance. But from the moment she started singing she had tears rolling down her cheeks. She was crying and singing incessantly. She would neither stop singing or crying. The breath pauses became moments to wipe tears and take breath with great difficulty as they had sobs blocking the flow of the song. The tears shocked Amma and Natarajan Mama alike. They did not know anything other than that she used to come and

138

visit NatarajanMama once in a while and took her to be a bye-stander in the next room. Kannan did not understand what was happening. Meanwhile a nurse came running from the nurse's station a few rooms away hearing Keerthana sing.

"She is in shock as her first stage performance as a singer had to be halted with a news of death of her mother," saying this she gave Keerthana a shot of sedative and slowly the song faded as she slipped into the induced sleep. Two attendants came in and lifted her by her arms and legs and took the bag of sleeping music to her room.

"Sir, the vehicle has come," said the young man dressed in formals. The drift back in memories were broken by his information. The little Kannan who saw the tears in Keerthana's eyes had the same pain when Kannan saw Henna's smile, who lost her ability to speak when she saw her dear mother die.

"We carry pain in our hearts so much that the pain remains even when the scars of the wounds which caused it vanish," Kannan thought to himself.

Trying to make a change in the lives of people who are distressed, Kannan awaits another day when people with more pain would walk into his room. Henna will speak to Bala soon.

28

Journey of faith

The temple arathi was reaching its crescendo when the whole Thiruvannamali temple was enveloped by the sounds of the bells. The lamps, the camphor, the incense and the flowers showered on the Thiruvannamalayan Arunachaleswarar, the deity in the sanctum sanctorum was giving a divine pleasure in the hearts of the hundreds assembled there. Kannan was standing near the doors of the main deity and his eyes were filled with tears of ecstasy, a feeling which can be described with no mere words for sure. The lamps lit behind the deity were giving a glow as if the Lord was present there to receive the lamps offered by the devotees.

Kannan took the prasad from the poojari and walked out of the temple. The evening winds made his salt and pepper long hair sway like the waves of sea. His beard and the vermillion on the forehead gave him a majestic look, like a king of the yesteryears living in the modern age. The fresh evening moonlight gave the smiling six-footer in white long kurta and white dhoti a strange peaceful glow. He was setting out on the Girivalam, the walk around the mountain, which is a customary practice in Thiruvannamalai.

Kannan walked fast through the busy streets and finished his darshans of the Brahma Lingam and Indra Lingam temples and moved towards the Karpaga Vinayagar temple, when the busy streets slowly gave way to the mountain road, silent, peaceful and serene. He walked through a small street to reach the Agni Lingam temple. Quickly had a darshan and walked out by the side of the Indra Theertham.

There were a few buses and cycles moving past him while he walked with his steady speed towards the outskirts of the town towards the Girivalam road. He had walked those roads many times before and the faith in his heart gave him all the strength to move forward. There were not many who were taking the Girivalam at that time. As the wind wiped a sweat from his forehead, Kannan thought of the fortunes he had in his life. The temples he had visited since his childhood. The ups and downs in his faith. The divine intervention in his life and the blessed moments for which he is thankful even today.

As a child Kannan was God-fearing to an extent of living a sagacious life even at a very young age. He hardly knew what worship is when he started spending hours in prayers. Time changed his thoughts with the life around him when in his teens wanted more than prayers and even had a fight with Appa.

"Why is it that every vacation we go to temples? Why can't we go somewhere nice?" Kannan asked Appa. Appa smiled and remained silent. Kannan now understands why he smiled. Those smiles just said one thing, "You will know whywhen the time comes."

Kannan smiled the same smile Appa smiled and walked towards the Yam Lingam temple. As he smeared the holy ash on his forehead and walked forward.

A small boy was walking holding on to his father's hand and Kannan heard him ask his father.

"Baba... hum paisa nahin denge to bhagwaan naaraz honge kya? (Would God be anry if we don't give money?)"

Kannan laughed in his heart as he had the same doubt when he was a small boy. Kannan waited to hear the answer, which turned out to be more hilarious.

"Shhhhh... badmash... aisa nahin kehte...paap lagega (Don't talk like that you fool. It'ssinful)."

We tend to silence the doubts our children have but not give them the answer or whether we know or not. Slowly enjoying the nightfall Kannan reached his next stop over for the walk which was at the Nirthi Lingam temple. The night pooja was being performed and Kannan was praying for Narayan when the mobile buzzed to life in his pocket. The vibration was felt and not heard amidst the noise at the temple filled with people.

Kannan walked out and took the call as he continued his walk.

"Appa, are you okay? How are you? When are you back?" Narayan was eager to know how his Appa was.

"I am fine. Just finished a quarter of the Girivalam. Praying for you."

"Appa, does your leg hurt now?" Narayan asked

"A little, but it's okay," Kannan replied, "I will finish the Girivalam and call you. Go have your dinner."

Kannan cut the call and continued his journey forward physically and backward in his mind. The leaves from the trees cushioned his walk forward but the time in his life, which hurt the most, came to his mind.

The young blood and the association with the extreme left thought his teacher Suresh Sir gave him a period of rational thought. Seeing God as a lie told to fool and scare people. Kannan turned to be an atheist against what he used to be during his late teens. Kannan's eyes filled with tears as he thought about those foolish days when he argued with those who had the faith and asked him to keep the faith in the supreme power. Kannan's phone rang again. He looked at the screen and the name flashed

"God's Gift" and Kannan answered. "Narayana, what now? I said I will call you after I finish."

"Nothing pa... just was worried about you." And he cut the call.

The bond between the aging father and the young son in his late teens was beyond anyone could understand. Kannan moved to the next temple, which was the Surya Lingam temple. As the night sky was getting darker, the full moon was lighting it more. Kannan walked forward and stopped at a tea shop and had a tea. Sipping it, he was thinking of the moments at Udupi temple during one of the vacations.

"Kanna," called the priest as Appa, Amma, Kannan and Akka were walking out of the Udupi temple.

Kannan looked back at the frail hermit with dark short hair and a thick beard clad in saffron smiling at him. All were surprised as Kannan walked towards the head priest in charge of the temple for that period. He was Swami Paryaya from Puttige Mutt in Udupi. A person never seen before, calling him by name and that did not astonish Kannan.

"Will you have lunch with me?" asked the saint.

Kannan smiled and agreed.

Those memories sweetened the thoughts hurt by the memories of being an atheist for a period later in life. Kannan gave the change and smiled at the tea vendor. His walk was to the next temple which was Varuna Lingam temple. Many temples crossed the minds of Kannan as he walked forward.

"Kanna, I did not know that I was pregnant when I was at Samayapuram temple," he remembered Amma's words, and the eyes that lit up when she said that. "I prayed for a baby boy at Guruvayoor and you are His gift to me." The talk with Amma echoed in his mind as he walked forward to Vayu Lingam temple.

Kannan swiped the screen to open the gallery and see some old pictures while he walked forward. In the heart of hearts, he thanked every happy moment in life. He saw baby Narayan's picture and smiled. God's gift, he said to himself, as a horse cart trotted beside him.

"Sir, savaari?" asked the horseman.

"No thanks," said Kannan and walked forward.

The speed which he started was slowly ebbing off as he reached the Kubera Linga temple. Kannan sat there for a while and drank some water from the stainless steel drinking water cooler, which had a list of donors name written on it in red paint. As he got up Kannan had the two remaining destinations in mind. The Idukku Pillayar temple and the Eesanya Lingam temple which would complete his this year's Girivalam. Slow yet steady steps lead him to the small temple which had an opening hardly that would let a baby boy through. The belief is that if you come through, it's more a rebirth and all your sins are atoned. Kannan went around and put his arm first through the opening. With great effort he started pushing himself through the opening.

"Saami, even bigger guys come through it. You can. Push," Kannan heard the voice of a roadside vendor who was standing near the temple. Kannan slowly pushed himself through when a hand held his outstretched hand and started helping him. "Who could it be?" Kannan thought as the hands felt so familiar. As he pushed himself through and came out through the opening Kannan saw a smiling tall teenager holding his hand.

"Narayana," Kannan called out in amazement

"Did not want you to do it all alone. I was just behind you," Narayan said with a smile.

Kannan hugged him, bearing the Idukku Pillayar (Ganesh) as a witness to the love between the father and son. The last stretch of 3 kilometers were devoid of thoughts and filled with smiles when Kannan put his arm over his son's shoulder and walked towards the last of the temples in the Girivalam.

"So you said you did not want to come and what brings you all the way?" Kannan asked mockingly.

"You." was the answer from Narayan.

Both of them walked towards the room after the darshan at Eesanya Lingam temple completing the Girivalam. The walk had made Kannan tired and slept off reaching the room, woken in the wee hours of night when he felt something cold in his feet. He opened his eyes and the misty eyes saw Narayan by his feet in the brightness of the night lamp. He was awake applying cream on the blistered legs of his Appa. The smile on the face of the two was similar to the divine emotion the previous evening which leave no words to describe.

Love is simply divine.

29

A wish came true

Love is not just lending a shoulder to cry. But for Kannan, his shoulders were the ones which got soaked in tears. The strong friendship which was built over a year of being together in class reached a moment so beautiful that Kannan realized that he liked Priya. He wanted to tell her how comfortable her presence made him. The smiles they shared, the moments they enjoyed despite the differences and fights they were used to as close friends. The studies were the second reason for Kannan to be on time to college. It was that his eyes kept searching for the one. A friend to whom he could talk to, share his thoughts and feel that the day was worth every moment it had in it.

There were evenings when the scooter wouldn't start until Kannan had not dragged it along walking with Priya till the bus stop as he would be better off talking to her till the time she boarded the bus or days when a full tank petrol would be called empty and he would lock the scooter and board the bus with her. There would be evenings when suddenly Kannan would have a realization that there is an assignment to be submitted and that would be the reason for him to quickly take a ride down to her house. To see her stand there at the door in her nightie with a smile. But he never thought whether it was love until that evening. When he wanted to tell her. He sat all night writing a message on a card he made to express his love.

The clock chimed 12 and Kannan was still working on the card with sketch pens, scissors and all his creativity to create the best possible card which will carry the message of love. His eyes were turning red with strain, but he smiled to himself thinking that the color of love itself is red. He wrote a note on a piece of paper. Not satisfied, tore it into pieces. Wrote another one. Still not happy. The process went on and on. After two hours, he was happy with what he wrote and it was almost five past two. He packed the card with the message on it with a smile and sealed it with a kiss on it. It was his heart, the feeling he had. He was feeling loved and filled with love. Slept with the pack of love under his pillow.

The morning sun invited him out to take a breath of fresh air. He went out and felt the morning breeze. Finished his prayers, morning chores and had a wash with a song in his heart. Shaved to look the best and a generous splash of his favorite musk after shave. Dressed in his best in his favorite denims and light full sleeve shirt. And thought about Priya telling him in a casual talk, "I like full sleeve shirts. It has something special about it."

Dabbed the perfume and wore an enviable smile on his face. Had his breakfast in a hurry and rushed out. He went to the parking and there stood the green scooter, his ride. Like the pig tails of a school girl the mirrors were waiting for Kannan. He checked twice in the mirror how he looked. That's when the thought flashed in his mind.

"Oops... the card."

He ran back home, rushed to his room, when Amma saw him run and asked, "What happened Kanna?"

"Nothing ma, my workshop record. I forgot it here."

He took the pack and hid it in the record and pushed it into the bag and ran to the scooter back. He kicked the scooter and it sprung to life on the roads. He reached the classroom to find Priya sitting on the third bench with her regular mates. Smiled and lightly waved at her. The presence of the lecturer was of least importance. Waiting from hour to hour for the best moment. The time seemed to go slow with him that day. It was lunch break and still it was not the best moment. The regular chit chats about movies, classes, and casual jokes were gulping the time away and still it was not time for him to take the pack out from the record, where it was hiding with his heartbeats pacing for the moment. Before the classes resumed Priya came up to Kannan and said, "I need to talk to you. Something special. Can you come home this evening?"

Kannan could not hide the smile in his heart. Smiled and said, "With pleasure.I will be there before you reach."

The rest of the classes where just hours flying like seconds for Kannan. He was waiting to hear it from her. The last hour was over and Kannan ran to his scooter. Hung the bag in the clip, kick started the scooter and raced it to reach Priya who was as usual walking towards the bus stop. He braked his ride and smiled at her.

"I will wait for you at your place. Should I take your bag too?" asked Kannan

"It's okay. You go. I have told Amma that you would be coming home. Have a cup of coffee and have a chit chat," she smiled and replied.

Over the years Priya's Amma and Kannan shared a special bond. They were more friends than his other college mates. They discussed everything under the sun. Kannan drove towards the moment with wind in his hair and love in his heart. He reached home, parked his ride and rushed to the door. Rang the bell and waited with his black sling bag on his back. Tall, well groomed for the day, Kannan was more than confident what Priya was going to tell him. The door opened and Priya's Amma was at the door.

"Come on in. Priya had told me that you would be coming. You have a seat I will get you filter coffee."

The small guest room and a study on the ground floor and kitchen bedroom and living on the first floor. Priya's house was a remodeled old-fashioned house partitioned to call it a separate home. Kannan picked the newspaper and was going through it. He seemed to read every line, but nothing made sense to him. He was still thinking about the time which is yet to come. He said to himself in his mind.

"Well Priya… I… I think…"

"No no… That's not how I should start."

"Priya… will you …"

"Nah …"

"I want you in my life… for…"

"What the heck."

Kannan kept searching for the lines and he thought, "Let her say what she has to. Maybe then I just have to give her this pack."

He took out the record from inside the bag and kept it by his side. He kept looking at his watch and waited for Priya's coming home. Her mother came with the coffee and started talking to him.

"So, what's special. Something tell me that you are very happy today."

"Yes ma. Nothing. Just like that I am happy."

She went on talking to him, but his eyes were only at the door. Half an hour passed and her father reached home.

"Well Kannan, Priya is coming. I saw her around the corner."

"Good evening, Uncle," Kannan greeted and his eyes went in search of her.

And there she was, tired by the ride and the whole day at college. But the smile seemed to be fresh. She threw the bag on the sofa and plunged herself into the chair out of sheer exhaustion.

"Amma ... coffee," said Priya in a tired voice.

Amma smiled and both her father and mother went upstairs. Uncle was talking about something at office to her Amma and the sounds faded. Priya jumped from the chair and grabbed Kannan by his arm and rushed to the study.

"Come come..."

Kannan's heart was beating faster than ever; he even forgot to pick the record that was lying on the sofa.

"Guess what? Anwar proposed to me and I said yesssss," she said with all the excitement Kannan had ever seen.

Kannan stopped for a second and couldn't believe his ears. His heart sank. He had no words. His throat went dry. His heart almost stopped beating. He felt choked. He felt as if he was freezing. Priya shook him hard and said again.

"Yes yes yes. Anwar loves me."

Kannan smiled and pulled himself back together again.

"Congrats. So your Black Yamaha is yours now," referring to the joke which they cracked when Anwar a senior student, Always at his best, dark complexioned with a rectangular gold frame glasses, mostly with his black jeans and white full sleeve shirts with folded cuffs, and drove past Priya with a smile every now and then. "So... calls for a celebration," said Kannan with a heavy heart. He wanted to burst into tearsbut couldn't. He saw the happiness in her face and was happy for her.

He smiled and said, "So party at Lords Cafe tomorrow. Call him too. Let's meet."

Her eyes were shining, smiles so full and shy, unusually shy. Probably that's what love does to a woman and to a man. Kannan was heartbroken but still wore a smile as he walked to the other room. Grabbed his record and pushed it into the bag and started leaving.

"Have to go to the temple. Tell Amma that I left." Kannan walked towards his scooter. As he was leaving he saw Priya at the door waving with a smile to her best friend, who still had the love hidden in his heart. Kannan rode waving back to her and before he reached home he parked he stopped by the side of the road. He opened his bag and took the hiding pack from the record. He opened it and read the lines he had written for her.

"I want to see you smile ... I want to see the glow of love in you ... I want to see your happiness."

And yes, his wish came true. He threw the card in the dustbin by the side of the road. Kept the record back in the bag and rode home still hiding the love, which he had for her.

30

Monsoon memories

It was raining and the drops of water fell into the room through the open window. The raindrops falling on the leaves on the potted plants made them dance in joy. The moist soil was giving out a unique smell of the soil. The evening sun had just set with its amber coat of colour giving way to the nights blue and the moonlight was slowly getting wet in the rain which was pouring as drizzles as if nature was whispering something - a secret. Kannan was looking out through the window since evening. He remembered rain has been a part of his life as a friend since childhood.

The days when he tore a centre page from the rough work notebook and folded it carefully as Raman Msama had taught him. He made a small paper boat and sailed it in the collected water in the drain and see it drift swiftly as more rain water was flowing through the drain than it could hold. The dinner which made his mouth water - porridge (Kanji) with lentils and roast pappads. The leaves of jackfruit tree folded by Appa to form spoons to drink the porridge. The dripping old tiled house and him and Akka running with vessels to keep the water from making the floor slippery.

He felt the rickshaw ride to his school when the light became red inside Thomas's cycle rickshaw with its red rain screens down. The days when he would run out in the rain and take his bicycle and take a ride before Amma would scold him for getting wet in the rain. The days when he would walk back from school getting wet in the rain. The wetness inside his shoes when the socks started getting damp and then wet with rain water. The bike rides to college when raindrops would feel like sharp needles falling on his skin. The sweet rain drops which trickle on the iron railings of the train compartment while travelling.

His thoughts were dropped when Amma called Kannan.

"What do you want for dinner Kanna?"

"Kanji, payar, roasted papadsand coconut chammanthi," said Kannan.

Amma smiled as she had guessed as much. Appa opened the door and walked in with his umbrella folded, dripping with water. He had gone to the temple and the usual song was there in his lips. He called out, "Kanna."

"Ooo ...," He answered and ran to the drawing room of the apartment. Seeing Appa drenched Kannan quickly took the towel which was carelessly dropped on the dining chair. Handed it over to Appa and looked at him.

Age had given him the grey hairs which came too early for himself. The smile was not moistened by the rain. He, his faith and routine were never stopped by any rain or sickness. It was another rainy season at home for Kannan, may be the last one for a long time and he kept looking outside while Appa continued humming the song and dried his wet hair. Seeing Kannan stand there and staring outside in a fixed gaze Appa turned to him and said, "Take some rest, will go to the temple tomorrow morning. Come have dinner."

Kannan silently nodded and went back to his room. The room was a mess with all the clothes folded and some here and there. Travel kits, books and packs of pickles and chips packed in cellophane covers.

"The gossips about my wife leaving me and the sad plight for the family sympathies from the sadistic relatives would get over soon. The case is in the court and will take at least ayear before everything would be over. Life just came to a standstill after four years of love in college four years of married life and separation," Kannan's thoughts made him look like a robot designed for packing. His heart was out in the rain with the wetness still in his mind. The dessert heat and sands would be his again after three years. This time he would be alone. New place, new job, new environment. The rain was washing away the thoughts troubling him since the day Priya left.

Amma walked to his room and said, "Cheer up Kanna. Leave everything to God. Everything would be alright. Past is past and you will be happy again."

Amma's words were like a caress on his heart, he smiled and locked the blue suitcase and went to the kitchen to see if some help was welcome. Dinner was over silently and the night silenced the house. The wake of the morning was the wake of a new chapter in Kannan's life. A quick temple visit and the trip to the airport was also shrouded in silence. Farewells were just shared with the eyes. As he walked into the airport, he kept looking back at Appa and Amma like a bird looks back after having the grains dropped for him and about to fly for the day. The flight took off and Appa and Amma were driving back home not talking to each other.

Amma was silently pouring her heart out like the drizzle outside.

"Don't worry. He can come for vacations or we can go to Dubai," Appa pacified Amma with his words.

As the flight took off to a new horizon rain was pouring still. The next rains would be waiting for Kannan for sure. He will be back to enjoy it. And whenever he thinks of the rain by the side of his window and the moonlight he would smile. The rain would shower in his heart for years to come as happiness in his heart.

31

The unfinished sketch

Kerala Express came to a halt and was like it was tired running all night stopped with a sigh of relief. The train which was supposed to reach Coimbatore last night at 8 reached late the next morning at 6 am. The hissing engine and the early morning Coimbatore station were like made for each other. The smell of the jasmine flower, hot idlis, hot vada and coffee was an inviting wake up call to those who were sleeping.

"Which station?"

"Coimbatore I guess," said Kannan, being a seasoned traveler by then.

He stepped out of the compartment. The smell of the metal inside the train was broken by the cool morning breeze at the station.

"Coffee... coffee ... chaai ... idli vadae ...," the usual station sounds was a welcome alarm for the others.

"*Oru* coffee" and Kannan bought a cup and gave the vendor his change.

He sipped the hot coffee with milk with sugar to sweeten up the morning and looked around. The station was not as busy as usual. He saw the hawkers here and there some selling cucumbers, flower, newspapers, coffee, tea, breakfast, idly wrapped in plantain leaves and newspapers porters trying to get the customers into the ongoing trains, some relaxing smoking a beedi. Few more hours and he would reach his destination, Ernakulam, back home Kannan thought to himself. Happy about his meetings in Delhi and the work he had ahead of him all the thoughts and the freshness of the coffee gifted him a smile. He looked into the compartment and most of them were still sleeping, not knowing what was happening around them.

"Train number 2625 Kerala Express from New Delhi to Trivandrum Junction will leave from platform no 3 shortly," the announcement came with the typical IVRS style with varying tones and a click.

The train hissed again and the horn was heard. The signal became green. Kannan quickly boarded the train. He saw people rushing into compartments here and there. He saw a bright faced young girl come running towards the gate he was standing.

She seemed to be a college girl returning home for vacations. In her bright yellow churidar she seemed to be a marigold running towards the train. Fresh and happy. Smiling in the morning sun. She had the smile in her face and the confidence that could beat the world. Kannan moved to the side and she quickly boarded the train and the train started moving. The train left the platform where the station guard was flashing the green signal. He went to his seat, the corner seat by the window. He saw the girl sitting on the opposite seat. She seemed to be so happy and was looking out of the window to the bright morning with trees whizzing past the train with the beat of the train sounds.

Kannan looked at her and thought, "Happiness. Is that her name?"

She looked at Kannan for a moment as if she heard what he thought and then turned away to her own world of happiness, looking out of the window and enjoying the wind in her loosely tied hair. She was hugging her bag as if it were her loved one. No books to read, no tiredness on her face, all that he could see was the excitement. He did not want to disturb her and he returned to the thick Robin Cook book he had bought from New Delhi station when he started back. Time to time, Kannan looked at the bright tingling eyes of the young girl sitting next to him. She was looking at the other passengers, listening to them talk; see the dresses they were wearing. It was more of observation than budging to their privacy. She would again return to the window sights of the morning village side. Kannan got busy with the medical mystery he was reading and didn't know when he slept of to the cool breeze by the window. He was woken up by the train halting at a station.

The girl smiled at him and said, "Sir, your book."

Kannan had dropped it while asleep. "Thanks," he said and took the book from her.

She was full of energy and seemed to be far away from the work troubles and pressures. Kannan wished he could take a small amount of the exuberance she had in her. He took his sketch pad and started throwing lines here and there like the hair on her face being tossed by the wind carelessly. He kept sketching the face and got engrossed in it. The hustle and bustle inside the compartment did not bother her in enjoying the happy moments nor Kannan who was sketching the lively marigold sitting on the opposite seat.

"Happy marigold," he thought to himself. He was sketching the eyes which were so lively and the train came to a halt at Palakkad Junction. She grabbed her bag and quickly got down. As she was walking away she looked at my sketch pad, smiled and walked away. Till he reached Ernakulam, Kannan was trying to finish the unfinished sketch and draw the eyes and fill her eyes with the energy she had. The life could not be captured after she had gone but it remained in his mind.

Years passed and Kannan never saw her again. Many days the journey remained in his head and from time to time he recollected the happiness in those eyes but never finished the sketch. His work kept him busy; home was another thought in his mind and ten year later Kannan was in Dubai with work. Every journey Kannan bought a new book and would finish it during the journey. Trips were reading time for him and flights, cars and trains were reading rooms for him. Centers of relaxation.

It was vacation and work together for Kannan this time and waited in the boarding area where he was to catch his early morning flight to Nedumbassery. He was sitting in the corner seat and saw a kid playing with a superman toy in his hand. The kid's energy and smiles brought back his memories of his Delhi-Ernakulam Kerala Express journey. He continued reading when the airport was busier than usual around him. It was going to be six and the flight boarding announcement was awaited.

The busy previous day and the night dinner meets had made Kannan tired. He did not know when he dozed off in his chair. He was woken up by the announcement and a lady standing in front of him. She smiled and gave him *The Princess*, the book he was reading, which had fell off while he slept. She was holding the kid by his hands and said "Sir, your book."

Kannan looked at those eyes. It was a moment of silence. He felt as if he has seen her before. Tried to recollect but in vain. The same eyes he had seen years back. Is she the "Happy marigold"? his thoughts sparkled. She gave the book and walked away. The silence around him covered him with awe and amazement.

"Passengers your kind attention please ...," he heard the announcement.

Some moments of silence still haunt Kannan. Who is she? Is she the same person? Journey of life does not have an end. The sketch book awaits another journey may be. But the life in the eyes taught him one thing. Life's paths change, take you places but the life and its happiness is from within and remains within you.

32

Sleepless night

Travel was both fun and work for Kannan. There were days when weekdays were regular job and on weekends he would leave on his bike in the morning and return with a smile on the face along with the dirt of the dusty roads late in the night as a part of his second job, rather a passion. The smile would be from all the accomplishments for the day, having trained his team far and wide in the multilevel marketing. It was a Sunday and Kannan set out on his work early in the morning.

Appa was out for his morning walk, Amma and Priya were sleeping. Sunday being a lazy day he knew they would wake up late. Kannan got himself ready in a pair of jeans and a jacket which carried the world for him. Each pocket was filled with something or the other for the day. The jacket was more of a pocket holder than a riding jacket. His choice of black for the ride was to hide the dirt and dust while he traveled far. He put his goggles on and got on the bike leaving a note on the dining table.

Will be late. Off to work.Love Kannan.

As he drove into the morning roads the trees shaded his face from the morning sunlight enough to warm a smile. Tshe streets were smiling with fragrant flowers, and morning had just started with its own set of activities. The bells of bicycles with newspaper rang a few bells, the milkman was also stopping by houses delivering milk at doorsteps. There were temple goers and the temples had their morning prayers on the worn-out speakers. Kannan drove past the city and got on to the highway. The smell of freshly brewed tea and vadas lured Kannan as he passed every small tea shop. Hard to resist he stopped by for a tea and snack. He saw a small boy by the side of the tea shop in rags. His smile was fading off in hunger and seeing his eyes crave for a snack, Kannan got him a vada and a tea. The smile which blossomed gave him more energy to set out with double the vigour. The day was fruitful and he met his team in Tamil Nadu. Marthandam, Nagecoil, Kanyakumari, the list seemed endless. It was already half past nine when he wound up the last team meeting in Kanyakumari.

"Sir. It was really interesting to see you handle your team," said Vimal, one of his team members.

Kannan smiled and was filled with joy to see his team active and revved up.

"Would you have dinner with us?" Vimal asked.

"With pleasure," said Kannan.

They went to Vimal's house, a small portion of a row house where the poverty had taken its toll. The happiness with which Vimal's sister served the hot idlis made it tastier. The sambar which smelled more of love than coriander, the idlis which looked more like smiley. The dinner was over a series of discussions on when the next meeting would be and what the plans were for the same.

Deep in his heart, he was so happy and excited and with the smile started back home. Kannan checked his watch and it was well past 11. The day's achievements, the small boy's smiles, Vimal and his team mate's love for him all kept him going and reached home by 1 in the night. He parked his bike and looked at the mirror on the bike. His eyes were sunk and the dirt had made them black as if he was returning from a boxing bout. But the sparkle in it was priceless. He was soaked in sweat but gave him the satisfaction of a successful day. He looked up to see the apartment lights were switched on.

"Who is awake at this hour" Kannan thought and punched the third-floor button of the lift.

The lift came to a halt and the corridor was dark. The light from home was seeping through the gap of the slightly open door. Kannan opened the door to find Amma and Priya in the hall room.

"Oh you did not sleep?" asked Kannan.

"What on earth do you think you are doing?" asked Amma angrily.

Kannan saw Priya's eyes wet with tears. He understood that the discussion between them would have been about him.

"The meeting got late and had dinner. So... I...," Kannan tried to explain.

"I don't want explanations," Priya said in an affirmative voice moist with worry and concern.

"How can you be careless like this? Don't you know we are here? Couldn't you just call once from somewhere?" Amma's started her firing with an arsenal of questions.

Kannan remained silent and stood there at the line of fire like a fallen soldier. The questions died down and night settled in another couple of minutes of scoffs, scorn and shouting. The night was not as comfortable as Kannan's heart wanted to share the success of the day but in return he went into the dumps mentally.

It was Monday morning and as Kannan woke up, he saw a cup of coffee by the bedside. Priya was getting ready to go to the temple, from where she would go to her parents' home and then to work. No exchange of byes or morning wishes were there for the day owing to the previous night. Kannan sipped the coffee and went to the hall room to check the headlines.

"Amma, I am going. See you in the evening," said Priya to Amma and walked away.

Kannan remained silent and was brushing through the news, when he felt a warm hand touch his arms. Kannan looked up and saw Amma. Fresh after a bath and prayers, but eyes revealed the sleepless night she had. She was smiling but still worried at heart.

"Don't feel bad," said Amma.

"I scolded you as Priya would feel left out if I don't share her worries and concerns. We were worried. But I saw the sense of achievement in the smile you had when you walked in."

Kannan could not say anything seeing the care which kept her awake and rendered her sleepless. There are moments in life when we do certain things for others and get hurt ourselves, little did Kannan know how difficult it was for Amma. He saw Amma get back to the kitchen where the morning breakfast was keeping Amma busy. Kannan kept the coffee cup in the sink for washing and turned to Amma with a smile.

"I am sorry Amma. Will try and avoid such situations," said Kannan.

The smile on Amma's face said it all. The day began with love and all the happiness of the previous day's accomplishments.

33

One more candle

The doorbell buzzed and Kannan opened the door to see a man standing there at the door with a package:

"Sir, Courier for you. Mr. Kannan Iyer?

"Yes," Kannan replied.

He signed the document with a smile and asked the courier boy who was in his red and yellow uniform, sweating as if he just had a shower, as he had been out in the sun.

"Would you like to have some water?"

He smiled and his eyes thanked Kannan in return. There was no verbal communication, but the gratitude was conveyed as Kannan handed him a cold bottle of water. The boy, who should be in his 20s, took the signed paper back and walked away smiling with a relief.

Kannan opened the grey pouch to see a gift pack in it. He opened the package and saw a purple colored aromatic lavender candle with a purple ribbon on it tied in a bow. There was a card in it from the sender. Every time Kannan sees a candle there are a million thoughts that rush to his mind. Thoughts about the time he spent in singing and fun with Akka during the power cuts at home, the candles that he lit in the church, the candles which he blew to celebrate his birthday, the candles which were lit to light the fire crackers for Diwali and the lamps for Karthika, the candle which lives for a few hours and finally burns out giving memories to him.

During his teens, the power outage was very common and all family talks happen during that time of the evening. As usual, the very punctual electricity board switched the power off in the area. Kannan happily jumped from his table as studies could wait another half an hour. He heard Amma call out to him.

"Kanna, the candle is on the fridge top. Careful."

Kannan tiptoed in the darkness to fetch the candle and heard Akka start singing a classical song.

Paripalayamam .... sree padmanabha murarae ...

This was a mode of the power cut entertainment schedules and a way to practice, when she is not busy with what she liked the most - studying. Kannan walked towards the dining room where Akka and Amma were sitting and the light of the candle brightened to dark room to reveal the two blessings in his life - Amma and Akka.

Akka was being trained in singing since childhood. It was a special music instructor who trained Pachai in singing. Tall, dark and slim young man, with thick hair combed back, long black beard and stern eyes. His forehead always had a white ash smeared in a thin line. The loose full sleeve shirt and white dhoti, on the back Hercules cycle with a green leather seat cover, made him look like a new age poor man's warrior. The sight of the music teacher, who looked more like dark complexioned Jesus with his long black beard and slim body, sent shivers down Akka's spine. Most often the classes would end up in a scene worth a mention. There would be a loud shout from Chandrasekhar, the music teacher.

"Where is *pa*?" when she misses a note in her singing.

The music notes would be all over the place and the leaves of the book flying around as if it were the fall and the pages were autumn leaves. Akka would be sitting near the harmonium which would have gone silent by then and Akka crying with her face covered after the thunderous shout. The chair would be empty and anyone could hardly see Chandrasekhar bang the door and fly out in lightning speed to his cycle and would pedal away in anger.

But for Kannan she was the best singer ever. Kannan would sit and admire her singing for a short while and try his luck in matching her in the song along with her, for which she would shout back and the whole story would end up in a fight between the loving brother and sister. But power cuts helped Kannan learn singing from one his best teachers his Akka - Pachai. It was with her he learnt about the ragas. She still reminds the Kadanakoodoohala raga which is a rag in the Carnatic stream which can even make the sad person smile. It was her notes that Kannan tried to trace and mimic and learnt singing.

Many years later, the power cuts were a common entertainment time at home, when both of them joined in singing classical and film songs, where in the darkness Amma would wipe her tears of joy listening to the two gems she had given birth to. But never tell them about her pride as she always believed they might be arrogant, if she praises them.

Kannan was reminded of the candle Thatha always lit in front of Alphonsa Amma's picture in his pooja, transcending the faith. The candles he and Amma lit before the St Antony's

Church for Appa, when someone had suggested that lighting candles at the church will help Appa get well soon. He thought about the pack of candles he lit before Mother Mary and Immanuel's church by the beach every night, till the morning he left for Dubai. There were no power cuts in Dubai, but still Kannan had a pack of candles always with him as they reminded him of his days, the memories and all the good things in life.

Kannan took the card from the box which held the candle and there was a note on it.

I was in Pondicherry and saw this candle. I thought of you. Spread light and aroma like this candle. Love Pachai.

Kannan's eyes were moist with tears of joy. Again, a candle which will rekindle the light of love and affection and spread the aroma of one of his first gurus, his Akka. Sure, candles have a duty to spread the light and shed light on those happy memories and whenever Kannan lit a candle his heart heard him and Akka sing together the famous Swathithirunal Krithi *paripalayalam sree padmanabha murarae* ... The carnatic classical keerthanam in Reethigowla, Akka's favorite rag.

34

My daddy strongest ...

The night was young enough for Kannan but the days of fun and frolic with Appa and Amma was beyond comparison and all of it coming to an end. The apartment became silent as everyone went to sleep. It was a sleepless night for Kannan. He tossed and turned around thinking whether he had missed something. What more needs to be done. Wheel chairs for Appa and Amma's comfort, tickets, time and lots of things kept coming back to him.

By the bedside table the table lamp was awake like a lonely tramp. The diary beside it waited for Kannan's hand to run on it and the pen to scribble down the precious memories. Kannan wrote on his favorite personal diary.

"Be it the fear of the dark, the fear of taking responsibilities or sharing and caring, throughout my childhood memories, Appa made me stronger and stronger by the day. Appa my role model. A strong man in all its senses who kept a smiling face even in grave worries. After many years it was during the surgery that Appa had to go through, it was for the first time

I saw him weak and fragile. But that was due to illness. Appa was never down even with fever as far as I can remember."

It's after five years since Appa and Amma came to Dubai. A couple of days short of a fortnight, days and nights just swept away time like the desert winds. Sun seemed to shine more than usual making it a long day of final rounds of shopping and spending time together. I held Appa's hands whenever possible with all the love and care as he used to walk me when I was small. Was he or was it me trying to recollect all those moments spent in smiles and laughs?

"Yes, my Appa is still strong. God save him from evil eyes."

Kannan thought to himself while looking at the ecstatic smile on Appa's face and continued writing with a heavy heart and a lumped throat. The worry that they are leaving left a heavy lump in his throat like never before.

"Day before yesterday, we set out on a journey close to nature for Appa to enjoy and lived all the moments which made them smile. I drove through Sharjah and Appa was happy to see the streets again where he used to take a stroll years back. Like a kid Appa enjoyed the sights of Ajman. We saw hundreds of birds there near the beach and he was smiling like a kid. At Umm al Quwain we felt the cool breeze in the afternoon. Lunch was at Ras Al Khaimah where I held Appa as if he were a kid who was with his mother. After lunch we had ice cream from Mc Donald's. Then a drive by the mountains to Masafi, then went to Fujairah and drove to Friday market. Saw the fruits and dates. I remember when Appa used to come back from trips with bags of fruits or yummy pastries for me and Akka."

"Then we had a special tea by the roadside. When I offered to stop for a tea he nodded like dudes would do on an off road adventure.

"Appa stepped out of the car and the wind pushed his hair and ruffled it. I always remember Appa so well kept, hair well-gelled to a style of his own. I did not think twice, put my hand out of the driving seat and combed Appa's hair and felt the truth - happiness is simplicity and nothing expensive, yet priceless. After a hot cup of tea, we drove back through the mountainous Dhaid roads to Sharjah and then back home. Driving for Appa through 6 emirates for 12 hours only thinking of the love shared, made me happy and my body tired.

"As we walked in to the house by 11pm, the night silence in the apartment was broken by our chit chat and it echoed in the sleepy corridors. We spent as much worthwhile time as possible as it was many years later we got to spend time together and the night was spent in packing the bags for Appa and Amma's trip back home."

His writing was broken by a shadowed dark figure near the bedroom door. It was Appa.

"Get some sleep, you have a long day tomorrow," Appa said to Kannan with a smiling face and a tired voice.

"Was just jotting down something. Hitting the bed now," Kannan replied.

That reminded him of Appa asking the same question when he used to sit late in the night back home.

"So what time is the flight?" Kannan checked again as if he did not know

"11.22," said Appa with a smile.

Behind that smile was the pain in the eyes of the father and son. Amma can cry but Appa. No, he won't. He is strong. As the adlib goes Kannan always felt, "My daddy is the strongest."

Kannan felt that he is considered a grown up by his Appa. It was more than any recognition he could receive in his lifetime. He bought all that could bring a smile to Appa and Amma's face. Smiles were being exchanged and time was flying too fast. Appa was never up so late, maybe the thought of leaving his son kept him awake. Amma worried about Appa's health and she was also going through the turmoil, whether to be happy about the happy 12 days or be sad about the last 12 hours with their son.

Kannan switched the table lamp off and darkness prevailed but for the salt lamp which burned throughout. He never realized when he dozed off to sleep. The morning coffee was accompanied by quick checks, locks, keys and the packing was done.

"Where are the house keys? I can't find them," Appa said.

The look on Amma's face was worth an award. She turned pale.

"Did you check the pouch?... Or maybe ..."

"No it is in the bottom of the travel bag."

The shift of expression was on to Kannan. Unpack the whole bag to retrieve the key.

Appa and Kannan quickly opened the lock and removed everything from the bag. There it was. The mystery of the missing key had been solved. Then it was repacking all over again. Kannan remembered how he used to pack his school bag. It was his turn to pack bags for Appa. Golden moments that appeared to be a gift from God.

It was time to go to the airport. Amma's eyes had started pouring the parting rain. Hugs were being exchanged at home. Luggage was loaded on to the car. The sky seemed to reflect the gloom. The morning sky had clouds so dark and sun was hiding behind them. Kannan with moist eyes quickly glanced Appa. He was okay. He felt again in his heart, "Appa is strong."

At the check in counter Appa passed the passport and tickets to Kannan and he gave it to the counter staff. The luggage was tagged boarding cards printed. The airport was busy as usual. But for Kannan the world seemed to be slowing down. His heart was sinking in the thought that they are going back to India. Why did the days go so fast?

"So take care of your health," Appa said smiling to Kannan.

He couldn't look at Appa as he was hiding the tears from them.

Amma spoke nothing and was trying to stop the tears that were on the verge of a fall.

The wheel chair assistants were waiting for both of them.

"Take care of them," Kannan quickly told them and took some money and handed over to them.

"We will," came the reply with a smile.

Kannan wished he was working there as the support staff and he could take them to the aircraft.

Kannan asked them to stop before they entered the immigration area. He bent forward and kissed Amma's forehead. Then turned towards Appa and kissed his forehead for the first time in his life. The expression of love towards one another was never so before. It was like the first rain of love which showered through their eyes. The world seemed to have stopped around them.

A drop of tear fell from Appa's eyes. All the strength seemed to melt away. Nothing more was spoken. Just the eyes remained in Kannan's mind. The drop of tear and the moment seemed to be the only thing he could see. From then on, every time Kannan thought about Appa he just remembered the eyes and the tear. All the fun and frolic were rolled into one tear drop which fell from his strong Appa. Or was it all the love Appa had for Kannan which took the form of one sweet tear drop. Yes, he was happy and Kannan smiled with moist eyes.

35

Touch, the home remedy

"Achoooo ..." his sneeze shook the apartment. And it sounded like a thunder.

Kannan smiled after the sneeze and told himself, "God bless you."

Being down with a cold or fever was not a common thing for Kannan since the time he left his stressful media career a few years back. Starting to enjoy life to its fullest, Kannan was not deterred by the fever and was enjoying the hot cup of coffee with ginger powder. For night it should be steaming hot kanji (rice porridge), with payar (lentils) and pappad, he planned.

"Have this cup of coffee. It's special and your fever will be gone in no time," Amma used to tell him in childhood days handing him the cup of coffee and dried ginger powder sweetened with palm sugar. The taste of the ginger, soothened his throat, the sweetness made it palatable, the coffee gave him the freedom from dullness, but what made it special was the mother's love which was in it. While the little Kannan in bed, had his coffee, Amma used to rub his forehead and ruffle his hair, while checking from time to time whether the fever was down. The touch was more powerful than any medicine in this world. For Kannan household medicines worked much faster than any English medicine available in the market then. Even now Kannan tries all the household tips and tricks to get better or to just remember those glorious childhood days. Though Akka is a doctor, she too loves to try out the so called "grandma's tips and tricks" the quick fixes for life.

But this time, when fever struck Kannan, he was alone at his apartment and the age-old techniques were gone, and replaced with instant ginger coffee powder, which lacked both, the taste and the love. Kannan sipped it and looked outside through his window. The evening sun had just started smiling the farewell for the day, giving the sky a new hue of red. There was a small bird at the window outside the glass looking at him, or he felt so. The other days, he never had the time to pause and look outside to the nature or the colorful skies.

"Is being sick a privilege??" Kannan thought for a while and started recollecting the past.

The time when he was on vacation to Thatha's place, the change of climate and food had given him a very bad stomach ache. Thatha had just finished his dinner and heard Kannan cry.

"Awwww... My stomach. It's aching."

Thatha looked at the clock. It was well past 11. He was concerned as all the nearby medical shops would have closed for the day. He went into the kitchen, took a steel tumbler, the typical coffee cup for any Brahmin house for the morning filter coffee. Put some kayam (asafoetida), hing as they call it in the north, in it and mixed it well with water. He ran back where Kannan was crying.

"Lakshmi, give this to Kannan," Thatha gave it to Amma. "It will cure the pain soon." And as he gave the tumbler to Amma, he would close his eyes and pray. Was it the love or the prayers, but the pain vanished and gifted the small Kannan a good night's sleep.

There were times Kannan remembered the touch which lessened the pain. When he had an accident and was at the hospital. The tears which dripped from Venki Mama's hands which wet his hands while he remained silent by the bedside. The warm hands of Appa on the forehead, when he would come and check if the fever is down and smile. How comforting a touch can be, only those who enjoyed it will know.

There was a moment in life when Kannan could give that touch of love and care to Appa, for once. Appa was to be hospitalized for a surgery, a couple of years back. Kannan reached the previous night and Appa was a bit tense with the surgery the next day. He was a person who would never think of taking rest or be concerned about not being well. He would have a wash and set out on his work even he was down with fever. All he wore is a smile, which still remains radiant in Kannan's mind.

The hospital was busy in the morning when they arrived. There were patients going out of the hospital with all the belongings after their discharge. There were people waiting to see the doctor, waiting impatiently. The people waiting for the lift, the nurses in their white sarees, the attendants pushing the stretchers on wheels, doctors running busy with their coat and stethoscopes as garland on the shoulders of the life savers. All that rush was not seen on Kannan's eyes. He just was holding Appa and looking at him as they walked to the room. The room was comfortable. When the admission procedures finished, the doctor came for check up before the surgery.

"So Gopal, how are we this morning? It will be over in an hour or so. Nothing to worry," said Dr. Akbar, the senior surgeon who was doing the procedure. He was about 5 foot 10 and with grey ruffled hair, curly and grey. His specs were on the edge of his nose, which would be praying to God that it does not fall of the ridge of his nose. Carelessly he adjusted the glasses from time to time. He smelt of smoke more than medicines, but everyone entrusted their lives as he was one of the best in town.

Appa silently smiled and said nothing. He was scared deep inside, but would never show it out, or rather should say that he never knew to express his fears or worries. The nurse walked in and gave the scrubs to wear for the surgery. Appa changed to the scrubs and laughed at the funny look as he was being taken to the theatre. He was asked to lie down on the stretcher. As the stretcher started moving, Appa held Kannan's hands tightly, as Kannan used to hold Appa's hands in childhood. There were emotions of assurance and hope being given in those looks and grip of the hands being held. Kannan smiled and told Appa.

"I am here, don't worry. Everything will be alright."

The surgery was over in a couple of anxious hours and he was moved to the post operative room. The nurse came up to Kannan and said, "You can see him now."

Kannan walked into the sterile post operative room. The room smelt of disinfectants and medicines. He saw the corner bedwhere Appa was under the influence of the sedatives and slowly recovering from the sedation. Kannan walked up to the bed and smiled at him, as he saw the eyes drowsily open a bit. Appa smiled back.

"There is a little pain, but I am alright," said Appa in slurred voice.

Kannan held his hand tight "You will be alright soon. Just need a few days of rest."

Kannan gently touched Appa's forehead and caressed it with love. He was being a mother to Appa for a moment, who lost his mother when he was just 27 days old. The mother's touch can do wonders, they say. But do they mean only mothers have that touch. May be. But for Kannan, that moment was realizing motherhood. The touch and care he got from Appa and Amma all these years found a vent to give back the same to Appa. The touch can make you feel better for sure. The father and son got time to exchange the love they had in their hearts for years, but never got a chance to express. The days taught them the magic of touch more than the medicines. For sure, touch is the best medicine: The touch of love, the happy medicine Kannan could give Appa on that day after surgery.

The medicine worked for Kannan in the form of mother's touch, the parting shake hand when Akka was leaving for US, the hugs from the friends after a silly fight which made things alright, the pat on the cheek with love from Thatha, the fond caresses from Ammamma, the touch of his beloved that seemed to melt away everything that worried him, the touch on the head by his teachers and elders as a blessing, the touch of a child with a smile that gives hope, the hi fi's, the touch of a friend on the shoulder telling him, we are with you, till the last cold touch, which no one has ever felt themselves.

The touch... touch of love... touch of care ... remains the best medicine for all ills. But a few medicines are no longer available as Thatha is no more to give the pinch of holy ash clasped between his fingers during his prayers, Amma is far away from Kannan to come and keep her warm hands on the forehead, Akka is in the US, too far to come and take care of him.

All through Kannan's childhood, he saw Amma's eyes fill up with tears when he fell ill. He saw the concern in Appa's eyes which turned red when he was tense. He saw the care Akka had when he was in bed. Thatha, Ammamma, uncles, all had hearts which cared for him. Now he was not feeling well and the warmth of the thoughts seemed to give him the coziness he badly needed when the big man curled up under the blanket like a little child in the bed. He would be hale and healthy cured with the thoughts of love for sure. To see the sun smile again in the skies.

36

Best teachers in life

The morning alarm ripped the silence in the room. 6 am. "Long day," he thought to himself. Quickly folded the Cafe Blanc filter paper cone for the machine and switched the machine on. The aroma of freshly brewed coffee filled the room. The pizza box was on the sink side of the kitchen. A dash of sugar in his coffee mug, which read "I am a foodies" and a quick stir, and begins the day with the mildly sweet warm black coffee.

The day started for Kannan with the usual browsing on the Internet and newspaper. The day seemed to be yet another day but all that he could see was Dr. Radhakrishnan's picture and a lot about teachers. He quickly checked the date on the calendar - 5th September. As any modern techno savvy guy would do Kannan searched the Internet and there it was.

5 September 1888.

The birth date of the second President of India, academic philosopher, Dr. Sarvepalli Radhakrishnan, is a celebrated day, where teachers and students report to school as usual but the usual activities and classes are replaced by activities of celebration, thanks and remembrance.

Google seems to be ready with the answer like a wife. An answer for everything. While whizzing past the headlines and his favorite Sudoku page, he drifted into thought which came to him as a flash.

"So many have taught me in schools and colleges. They are not just the teachers who taught me life. Who all contributed to my stature in life today?" Kannan thought.

The awards and medallions adorned the red stand on the wall. It seemed a bit crowded there on it. But the thought grew on him. The empty room started filling up with faces in the mind of Kannan. He took the laptop, unplugged the charger and took it to the chair and switched it on. The windows signature tune would be the alarm for the person living next door. He opened a notepad and started.

"Appa and Amma," he keyed in to his laptop. "My Thatha. He told me many stories which taught me values. Yes, Ammamma. She taught me the basics of singing. My first school...." thoughts started pouring in like a storm and names started popping up like the lights in a festive mood.

The list went on and on with some names correct and some which he had forgotten.

"Varghese Sir, Natarajan Sir, Gangadharan Sir, Carrie Sir, Vijayan Sir ..."

He lost interest in the mundane news of the day on the papers. The TV was airing the live breaking news from around the world, the hot coffee that lured him to wake up from the leftover slumber, now seems to be waiting to be sipped, and getting cold in the cup.

Names whirred in his head like a machine and started keying them in as fast as possible.... 60 names ... now 83, more ... more... yes 120... and within an hour, he keyed in a huge list of over 200 people who made him what he was today. Kannan looked at the coffee, took a sip and found it to be cold and slugged down his throat.

He opened his Facebook account and started with a smile on his face.

"To all the dearest teachers in my life who made me what I am. On Teachers' Day I would like to thank each and every one of them."

Clicked the photo icon and uploaded the picture collage he had made out of the list of teachers names. "Post", and there it was.

"Is it all the likes and comments that I want? I need to thank at least one of them personally." He searched his phone and got his friends number.

"DaLinu. Do you know our class teacher TT Albert Sir's number? I wanted to call him. After school have never spoken to him."

"Yeah. Remember the cane he used to carry?" Linu said abruptly.

Thoughts were exchanged over 10 minutes discussing the interesting school times. Time seemed to melt away with the excited hyper talks about the teachers, the pranks, the fun, the food, the lunch time and everything under the sun then. Linu stopped in between and said.

"Kanna, here is the number."

Kannan carefully noted the number on a notepad on the table. "Ok da. Thanks. Chat later," and hung up.

For a second, Kannan relived those moments. He felt refreshed. "Albert Sir was so strict and is he the right person to call today? Should I? will he remember me? It's been so long, over 20 years. He might not remember me...." he kept thinking for some time.

"Bzzzzzzz" the vibrations of his smartphone made him realize the whole lot of people who have started liking and commenting on the status he had updated a while ago.

Kannan took his phone and dialed the number. There was a pause and silence. Anxiety. Excitement. He did not know what to say and how to start. The phone was ringing and there was silence on this side of the phone.

"Hello, Albert here," said a faint tired voice.

The whole hustle and bustle around Kannan settled down. All that he heard now was that voice over the phone. The voice seemed to be frail and weak. Not the stern voice of the teacher who came to the class in classy trousers and well-pressed full sleeve shirts. The word silence used to reverberate in the corridors of the school when he demanded it. And it used to be silence then on in the class.

"Is it the same Albert Sir I know?" Kannan thought for a moment before he replied. "Sir... I am your student Kannan."

"Kannan? I faintly remember a few. Sorry I am not able to place you. But how are you? Where are you?" Kannan heard Albert Sir's weak yet excited voice. He seemed to be happy to hear me, Kannan thought.

"Sir, you were our class teacher. You taught us English and...," Kannan gave many instances for him to think back about his younger days. Some made him smile and some left him silent. Those series of smiles and silences gave the warmth to the voice. Kannan heard the long breaths on the other side of the phone. The clock ticked in the room, which seemed to slow down for the teacher and student to travel back in time. Every other moment Kannan wished Albert Sir could place him in the huge list of students.

"Yeah, I do remember the bright-eyed boy, with big ears and .... and ... you were in the band troupe ... right?"

Kannan was delighted, "Yes Sir, I was."

"Ah. Now I remember you," said Albert Sir. There was a mellowed excitement, only affected by the age and loneliness.

"Oh I am so happy that you called. I am retired now and not keeping well. So nice of you to have called. Where are you now and what do you do?" Albert Sir talked in a slow and steady pace.

"Sir, I am a consultant. Now I am in Dubai. I write too, and it's the language you taught me that made me what I am today."

The whole world around them seemed to smile at them. The air conditioner in Kannan's apartment, took the chance to blow a cool breeze as if to celebrate this joyous moment of accomplishment.

"And son," he continued, "I know I have been strict with your kids. It's just that I wanted you to be much better than you could imagine. Don't keep it in your minds."

There was the silence which was not commanded but fell from the heavens. Kannan could feel Albert Sir in tears. Was there a drop of tear in his own eyes too. Yes, there was.

"Please call me and do come home sometimes when you come down to India. I am alone here.My wife passed away a few years back and sons are abroad," Albert Sir said. "And thanks for calling."

The click on the phone that cut the call was like the button of a remote to the world. The breaking news seemed to go silent. The comments on Facebook did not attract him. The world seemed to be silent in all its respects. He slowly walked towards the sofa and took his laptop. Keyed in a line as his new status update.

"The best teachers ever - Age and realization". Post.

Kannan did not want to look at the post or comments or the scandals posted on Facebook thanks to Zuckerberg. He looked at himself and smiled. took the phone and dialed again:

"Da bro Linu. I need more numbers. Will send you the list."

37

Lesson about rich and poor

"Teachers are not always found in school. People around you teach you a little. Teachers in schools teach a little and life teaches you the rest," all were gathered around Mahadevan Thatha and were eagerly listening to his soft yet heavy voice, while he finished the magic trick with cards for kids.

His voice had something divine about it. Six-footer, always preferring to wear white shirt and white bleached dhoti, no because of the choice of color, but after his retirement, he had means enough for just a pair which adorned him every other day. He walked with a little hunch owing to old agebut remained healthy all the while owing to the distances he used to walk with ease. He never had any great wishes. His smile on the face with the cataract removed eyes and thick glasses, the color of shining oak wood. Dark yet attractive complexion, exactly opposite to his brother the fair Sivaswamy Iyer, Kannan's Thatha. He and his wife Seethalakshmy, who lived in Kottayam, were never blessed with children, but he was blessed with a heart which always loved tiny tots.

Kottayam Thathi as Kannan and Pachai called Seethalakshmy Ammal was short in stature, dark in complexion but the dazzle of her age-old diamond studs and nose pin was characteristic with her regular silk 9 yard green silk saree she wore. More attractive was the crimson red kumkum she had on her forehead and the smile she always wore on her lips. Kannan was dearer to Mahadevan Thatha and Kottayam Thathi than a son, though he was Sivaswamy Iyer's grandson. He used to spend as much time he got with children around him. Kannan and Pachai took pride when all their cousins gathered around him to see him makes cards vanish from the lot with tricks of Mathematics. The way he taught algebra to the elder ones, played with the younger ones and told them interesting facts about places and temples far and wide.

As he bid farewell to Amma and walked his way towards the boat jetty, Kannan and Pachai were sad and were hoping to spend more time with him. He had his long black umbrella and a small black leather bag which had his other pair of white shirt, a dhoti and some documents and the little cash he would carry.

"Amma, when will Mahadevan Thatha come again?" asked Kannan as usual.

"Very soon if you study well and be a good boy," Amma gave him the usual answer.

His visit would leave a lot to think about and take to the school where everyone would flaunt their newly learnt tricks and techniques in Mathematics. He was a parallel university to the children till Appa got a job in Kollam and they moved to Trivandrum. For months Mahadevan Thatha had not visited them. Kannan would inquire from time to time about him and Amma would be busy in kitchen when she would tell him about the mail Thatha had got or Appa had got from Mahadevan Thatha. For months there was no news about him. It was a holiday and Kannan was playing in open balcony in front of the upper portion of the house in the colony, where they stayed. From a distance he saw Thatha walk hastily. The same snuff colored shirt, with sweat making the holy ash grey like mud smeared on his forehead. He was sweating profusely and gasping for air. He sat down on the stairs in exhaustion. Kannan stopped playing when he heard Thatha call Amma.

"Lakshmi," and Amma came running to her father sitting on the steps.

"Appa, why are you sitting on the steps? Come in," she said.

"No, I can't," said Thatha.

Amma was not able to understand what had happened or why he was saying so.

"What happened?" she asked looking at Thatha whose shirt had turned darker with dripping sweat from his body, eyes red with tears and voice dull and grief stricken.

"Mahadevan... He is gone," said Thatha in a broken voice.

"Where? Mahadevan, who?" owing to the shock, Amma could not understand anything.

"My brother," and tears started rolling down from Thatha's eyes.

He could not say anything. Amma's eyes also started pouring the grief out in tears. She went inside and got a glass of water for Thatha. He lifted the glass up in the air and poured the glass of water into his mouth. The sound of water being gulped was heard loud and clear. Kannan could hear Thatha tell Amma with his sobbing voice breaking at times.

189

"I want to see Mahadevan for a last time. But if I take a train I wouldn't be able to reach on time. I tried but... Can you lend me some money? Then I can take Raju's cab and reach as fast as possible," asked the desperate father to her daughter. Thatha sat on the steps with his hand on his wet forehead and Amma went running inside. She rushed back with the money and turned to Kannan.

"Go get changed," Kannan knew that there was something wrong, but could not really understand what was happening. He got ready and went with Amma and Thatha. Got Raju's cab and Venki and Swaminathan, Amma's brothers joined them. They were silent till they reached Mahadevan Thatha's home. The silence was broken only by the sobs and clearing of throats. Kannan remained silent, understanding the gravity of the situation.

Raju's black and yellow Ambassador taxi stopped at a house on the steep downward roadside enough for a car. They got out and Kannan saw a whole lot of people standing there. They were all either silent or talking in hushed voice to each other. Women were sitting in the small dimly lit room inside and crying with Kottayam Thathi.

"When was it?" An old man who walked in asked another person standing near the gate.

"Early morning. In sleep. Lucky man. Did not suffer at all."

"I met him last evening too," came another reply from the next person.

Eleven year old Kannan did not know who they were but was slowly coming to terms with the fact. They walked in where Mahadevan Thatha's body lay on the floor covered in his favorite white colored cloth. There were two pieces of coconut with wicks burning in them. There was a vadhyar wearing his dhoti in a traditional style talking to Thatha for a while. Kannan was looking around and was feeling stuffed in his chest. He has lost a teacher in his life forever, he will never again teach him math or the tricks or tell him about the important temples and places. Suddenly he felt a hand on his shoulder and Kannan turned towards the familiar voice of Thatha.

"Go have a bath and wear this dhoti and come."

Kannan took those words as the words from the supreme, asked not what, why or anything else. It was evening and the cold water from the well was poured over Kannan's head, who felt the chill to be less intense than the chill inside his heart on the loss. He reached the front of the house where Mahadevan Thatha's body was being lifted by four relatives. The vadhyar came and gave a small piece of green stem of a plantain leaf with cloth dipped in ghee and lit like a torch.

"Hold this and walk in the front."

The entourage of people walking towards the crematorium walked behind him. Kannan climbed the steep slope upwards towards the main road. Every step was difficult but he moved steadily.

An old lady who was standing by the wall near the road where the body was being taken by was heard talking.

"Poor Mahadevan. He has no sons or daughters and his brothers grandson is paving way to heaven with the ghee torch."

Kannan's eyes rolled out the tears which did not know to flow out expressing his grief. Thatha moved Kannan and Venki brought Kannan back from half way from those who went the crematorium. Those words of the old lady were a lesson in the traditions of those who had kids and those who did not.

"Teachers are not always found in school. People around you teach you a little, teachers in schools teach a little and life teaches you the rest," Kannan heard the night skies speak to him in Mahadevan Thatha's voice while they drove back home.

"Having children was not riches for Thatha and not having them had made Mahadevan Thatha poor," Kannan thought. A few nights the thoughts lingered in his mind. A firm mind was being molded by time in Kannan. Mahadevan Thatha would be an inspiration for him with the beautiful memories, whose death taught him one more lesson about what rich or poor meant otherwise for the society.

38

And time melts away

"Passengers your attention please,"

The flight had landed and the wait was getting more anxious. The announcements, cab drivers waiting for their turn, the coffee vendor, the busy morning newspaper stand, the air crew and the cleaners wiping the floor, the sounds of the cars moving. The airport receiving area was a bustle of activities. He was seeing his mother after a long time.

"Time please," the person standing next to him asked.

"6:55," he said quickly looking at his watch.

"Would the long-haul flight have been comfortable? Did she sleep off in the flight? How will she manage the luggage?" such questions pestered Kannan's mind.

He quickly sipped the last few drops of coffee with the leftover wet sticky sugar in it giving it a shockingly sweet taste and rushed towards the gate where the passengers had started getting out. He saw his Amma coming out of the gates. Her eyes were searching for her son among the crowd impatiently waiting for their loved ones.

"Did she see me? Oh how could she miss me?" He thought to himself.

He saw the smile on her face and understood that she has seen her son. He rushed through the crowd and took her trolley and gave her a quick smile and asked.

"So how was the flight? Everything fine?"

She looked at the grey hairs, the tired looks, times indelible marks on her sons face. He has gone thin than before. Is he alright? Does he have food properly on time? she thought to herself and quickly replied.

"Oh yes. It was very comfortable. You came alone?"

"Appa wanted to be at home and your Badhra is busy preparing breakfast for you… your favourite appam and stew," he said smiling.

The images of him as a kid flashed through her mind quickly. The bright eyes, big ears, black thick hair, the dirt on his shirt when he comes home after playing. It was an array of images that flashed in her. Was it heart or the mind? She never knew. She wanted to ruffle his hair as she used to do when he was a kid. He has grown up and would not be liking if I treat him like a kid. I should hold myself strong. She decided.

The morning wind was cool and the pulled down windows of the car let in the moist wet aroma of the sand drenched in the previous night's rain. The soothing wind relaxing after being inside the airtight aircraft for over 6 hours. Amma was tired and was trying to keep herself awake.

"We are buying a farm in Tamil Nadu. It's good, and the talks are on. We got a good price. They were asking for 90 but settled at 75." He went on and on.

She did not know when she dozed off into a light sleep and all that she could remember was the wall behind her kitchen at home. She saw herself stand there and talk to Geetha.

"Yesterday I went to Kannan's painting exhibition. It was nice. He paints so much, he does well. Vijayan sir said he has a bright future. He sings too. But I want to get him trained in violin. He is smart."

Geetha was listening to her smiling, which was usual to her. Every tea time, their gathering place was the green mold spread small wall which separated the two houses. Ramu and Shamu were small and they would be seated on the wall while they talked to each other every other day. They used to share their small happiness and sorrows over a cup of tea by the wall.

"I was there too, he is good," said Geetha.

They went on and on sipping the tea about their children.

"Here comes the star," said Geetha when she saw 9 year old Kannan run towards them.

Amma abruptly stopped the talk and looked towards him and said, "You only know to play and make fights. See how dirty your clothes are. How can you be so irresponsible? see Ramu and Shamu. They are so well groomed. Learn something from them."

Her harsh wordsslowed the small artist down. Kannan smiled at Geetha Chechi and waved at Ramu and Shamu and walked into the house through the kitchen door, head held low.

"Kids will get spoilt if we appreciate them in front of them," Amma said softly to Geetha.

She went inside to find her son tired after all the playing and fights with his cousins.

"What happened? Are you all right?" she asked Kannan.

"Amma," he said softly "Can I lie on your lap for sometime?" he asked her.

Amma was woken up by the screech of breaks. She woke up to see Appa standing there smiling at the door.

"Back to square one," she said. "I am back to my routine"

The opening of the baggage and the talk and food all took away a good amount of time. After the lunch Kannan walked towards Amma and asked her.

"Is everything alright at Akka's place?"

She went silent and after a short while she said, "She is fine."

The silence spoke a thousand words to the mother and son. Appa had gone to sleep and Badhra had stepped out for her meetings scheduled for the afternoon.

"Amma," he called out softly, "Can I lie down for sometime on your lap?"

She saw the same 9 year old Kannan again before her. Head held low. Tired after his 31 years of life from then. Amma smiled and hid the tears that were about to slip down through the corner of her eyes. The silence was peace for them. The air condition broke the silence but was just not heard anymore. Years of tiredness and time seemed to melt away on the mother's lap when the old hands ruffled his hair.

39

The best award ever

It was another lonely weekend for Kannan. As everyday his day started at 4 am. The alarm was waiting to be touched by him and silenced with a pat on its head. But as usual the alarm was late and Kannan was awake. The alarm went off with the touch and a lazy weekend for all was an active day for Kannan.

Making coffee, making toast and eggs for breakfast, checking mails, his canvas, the colors, with or without anyone around him, Kannan was busy till noon. Age was not a factor which kept him from trying anything new. At the age of 40, he would look 60 and be active as 20. The loneliness never made him think about what would happen tomorrow, but always found inspiration from the past. He was flipping the newspaper in the hot summer afternoon and Dubai summers burnt the skin of those who ventured out. He was going through the cinema page and saw the list of new movies.... one grabbed his attention.

Happy AsCan Be. "What a title," Kannan thought. He had the passion for movies since childhood. He got dressed finishing his lunch and grabbed the car keys from the table. The parking was scorched with heat, but his smile was warm as a spring morning. He whirred the engine and drove off to the nearby mall.

Single cinemas gave way to multiplexes, multiplexes to home cinema and satellite on demand movies to the cinema on the wrist with gadgets improving day by day. But the ways of expressing thought in movies remained with a handful of film makers, who made it a point to entertain the audience. Kannan parked his car and rushed to the cinemas, glancing at his watch from time to time for messages and time. He walked up to the counter greeted by the smiling Philippina, who punched the tickets out after confirming the seat.

He walked towards the hall looking at the posters and cut outs for all the movies being played there. The smell of freshly popping corn, the air freshener in the walkway, the smell of chestnuts, corn and the cotton candy. It's a real pleasure being at the cinemas. He checked his ticket and saw the Cinema:7 doors welcoming him for a treat.

"Happiness as can be ..."

As he entered the Cinema greeted by the freshness of the aerosols sprayed in the hall, he was reminded of the pleasure of cinemas all through from the past.

Thoughts of Venki, his uncle a movie buff and his love for cinemas, watching *Beautiful People*, the movie from the front rows with school mates, watching *Enakkul Oruvan*, another Kamal Hassan movie with Venki, watching *Vandanam*, the movie with just Appa in the stand alone Ajantha Cinema, when Amma and Akka got angry that the balcony tickets were sold out and those available were only first class. Kannan smiled at that thought. His journey back in time had some more time left, as there was more time for the movie to start. He thought about watching *The Mask*, when he had to walk out after a fight with Priya in the theatre. Introducing the Disney Movie *Finding Nemo* in 2003, to watching his own movies in the cinemas a few years back.

It was during one such movie night out that Kannan understood the unsaid love between him and Appa. Kannan's craze for movies and media had always worried Appa. From a conservative and orthodox family, cinema was considered a taboo indeed. Though he liked movies, the thought that his son's life might be spoilt with the vices of the industry worried him more.

"You are an engineering graduate and you know what to do. Up to you," Appa's words echoed in Kannan's mind when he thought about those days, when he wanted to be in media and movies like any other youngster.

Appa always remained silent on all major issues pertaining to Kannan's life, but kept his fears and worries in his heart. But one issue he spoke once to Kannan was in a few words

"Why media? You can do much better otherwise."

Every look after that statement for years mentioned his concern to Kannan. Years passed and Kannan had been doing well with a TV station with his interview shows and morning breakfast shows.

Years later, Appa had visited him for a few days on the way to his visit to US, to be with Akka and her kids. And it was just another weekend movie night out with Appa. As they were waiting for the hall to be vacated by those who were at the previous show and old man came running to Kannan. He was tall, spotting a grey beard, the strings from his spectacles went down and behind his neck. He seemed to be a seasoned professional from the striped blue shirt with the white cuffs, those which you wear as the inner for a suit, his tweed trousers and shining black shoes.

"Sir, I am Raghav Nambiar. Are you Kannan Iyer," asked him with curious eyes and an excited yet soft voice.

He was all excited to meet Kannan in person. His excitement could be felt standing next to him and did not notice Appa standing next to them.

Appa was looking at both of them as if he were the line referee at the Wimbledon left to right and right to left.

"Yes sir, I am," replied Kannan. "Pleasure meeting you."

"Sir, I saw your interview last week," he continued with smiles and adjusting his slipping glasses from time to time.

"Thanks," replied Kannan with a smile and a sense of satisfaction, "Hope you liked it."

"Oh. I can't explain. The questions, the way you handled it... the ... the ...," he kept searching for words to express his hearts feelings like a school boy searching for the next words of the answer he was asked for by the teacher.

"Thank you, sir.Thank you.All by God's grace," Kannan cut him short as he saw people had started entering the cinema.

Pointing to the cinema hall Kannan continued.

"Well I think it's time for the movie to start and my dad is here with me," Kannan carefully gestured with his right hand towards Appa.

He turned and looked at Appa with awe, paused for a moment, took a deep breath and quickly took Appa's hands in his.

"You are Kannan's father!!" asked Raghav still shaking Appa's hands. He had clasped Appa's hand snuggly with both his hands.

Appa just smiled and nodded. "Yes.Kannan is my son."

For a moment Kannan saw a glitter in the moist old eyes, which he had never seen before. Kannan looked at Appa and the old man for a second. The time froze that moment and Kannan's mind swirled in that moment like a butterfly. The feeling which he had then could never be put in words. Coming back to the moment, Kannan quickly wished good night to the old man, who was still smiling, to have met Kannan. He walked awayand kept looking at Kannan and Appa as he was walking out of the cinema area. Kannan saw Appa also looking at him with a smile in his eyes.

"Shall we go?" asked Kannan.

Appa was silent as usual, but his silence had a sigh of approval in between. He kept his hand on the back of Kannan as if he was taking Kannan forward and he heard his father's heart say, "I am proud of you my son."

That day Kannan did not see the movie on the screen but his mind kept playing the moment when Appa's eyes were shining and smiling. Kannan thought about the cinema intermissions back in his childhood days when Appa would pat his back, keep his hand on the small of Kannan's back, take him to the cafeteria and share his coffee on the saucer. The times were different, but Kannan still wanted to share the cup of coffee from Appa who would pour a little from his cup to the white saucer and hand it carefully to him. And when looking at the vapours from the coffee, Appa would take the saucer full of coffee and blow it cold enough for Kannan to sip and smile.

Those moments at the cinema were the best ever in Kannan's life. Since then Appa never asked him "Why media?" The smile on his face was worth more than any awards in the whole wide world for the little he could achieve.

Happy AsCan Be the movie title appeared on the screen and Kannan thought to himself, "Does life have subtitles for thoughts which appear on movie screens."

40

The first stage

It was yet another event in Kannan's life and Narayan was on stage for the first time. Kannan had his usual set of butterflies in his stomach. The fear and the apprehension had kept him going all these years were there when his son was on stage. The stage always beckoned again and again since childhood. Kannan spent hours to write the speech for him on Teachers'Day for Narayan. The pride he had when Narayan rehearsed his lines with style. He saw the smile on Narayan's face when he was rendering his lines to perfection.

Kannan remembered the first time he was on stage when he was in his upper kindergarten. He was enacting a play as the king in *The Sleeping Beauty*. Seema played his queen, Roshini was a fairy and Sheena was the princess. Kids of the same class rehearsed the play over and over again and the day arrived when the play was to be staged. The orange cape, red silk dress and the shoes with the silver lining all gave Kannan a smile which was beyond compare. He went on stage and played his part to the fullest. For years he kept looking at the pictures with pride. Amma was there to see the play, but never expressed her joy thinking it would spoil him.

The next time was when he was in his Class 1, when he was to give a speech on Teachers'Day. The speech was written by Kottayam Thatha and he took pride when Kannan rendered those lines.

"Dear parents, teachers and my dear friends. I would like to tell you about our teachers, who make us what we are...," Kannan had learnt those lines by rote and said as if he understood all that he was saying. Kottayam Thatha in his white shirt and dhoti was sitting eagerly to listen to his brother's grandson speak so well. Kannan saw the tears in his eyes when he completed the speech with those two magical words, "Thank You".

"Kottayam Thatha, did I say it right?" Kannan asked.

"Yes Kanna, you did." He smiled, wiped the tears of joy with his hands and hugged him.

The day when Kannan was to deliver his speech had arrived, but Kottayam Thatha had to leave. Kannan waved goodbye to Thatha the previous evening. As he was leaving, he asked Kannan to say those lines again and Kannan stood on the steps and said it with style to see Kottayam Thatha's eyes fill with joy.

It was Teachers'Day and Kannan was at his best. The red and black chequered shorts and the red tie with the school badge, hair cut to perfection and groomed like an army officer at his best. Kannan looked at the mirror many times before he went to the dining table to have his breakfast quickly before rushing to school. Akka was already at the table with her cream top, blue skirt and hair braided well in two pigtails on the sides tied with black ribbon.

"Amma, give me breakfast quick," said Kannan.

"Coming," said Amma.

Kannan held the piece of paper, which had the script, in his hand which Kottayam Thatha had given him. He was reading it over and over again with a smile.

"What is that?" asked Akka.

For a second Kannan felt blank. Then replied.

"I had told you. I am giving a speech for Teachers' Day today. Are you not coming?" Kannan asked eagerly.

"No we also have something in our class," replied Akka quickly finishing her breakfast.

"Amma," called out Kannan.

"Yes Kanna," was the reply from the kitchen.

"Are you not coming to school today to listen to my speech?" asked Kannan.

"I don't know. Have loads of work. Appa also has given me a lot of work. I have heard you say the speech so many times," said Amma as she came to the fining table from the kitchen wiping her sweat from the forehead with the back of her hand.

Kannan felt sad and his face did show it.

"Now don't sulk. Be a good boy. I know you will do well," Amma said.

Kannan folded the piece of paper and put it in his shirt pocket. He finished his breakfast and rushed to school.

The festivities added color to the same premises Kannan and his friends spent all the time. The steps of the school turned to be the place where the stage was put up and the back drop read "Teachers' Day 81". All the students from different classes walked to the corridor which was the venue for the event. There were parents and other elders too, who were there to witness the festivities. Kannan looked at the stage and there were butterflies in his stomach, which was a new feeling for him. He wanted to do his best and there was the feeling, "What if I go wrong?" Kannan prayed hard and was waiting for the name to be called.

"Kannan ... One B." The speakers boomed as the crowd stood there listening. It had teachers, his classmates, his school mates, their parents and so many people. Kannan stepped on the stage with a smile. There was only one thing in mind when he was on stage. How happy Kottayam Thatha would be if he were there. He just thought of those eyes with tears of joy. Kannan walked to the mic, which was set to his height. He adjusted it with his little hands and started.

"Dear parents, teachers and my dear friends...,"

With a thumping heart Kannan finished his speech in a flow, not even stopping for a doubt, as Thatha had trained him so well with the lines. As he finished Kannan said,

"Thank You"

The corridor of the school, overflowing with the sea of people, burst into applause seeing the little one finish the speech in confidence and style. The claps gave Kannan the sense of satisfaction and happiness. He was full of joy. His eyes searched for a familiar face among the crowd. The eyes looked far, kept looking for his loved ones, kept looking for Amma, Akka or Appa. No one was seen. He stood there by the side of the stage and each time a performance finished he saw the child's parent come and lift him up with smiles galore and hug him. Kannan kept looking if someone would come and hug him too. His face dropped like a flower in the midday sun and his heart sank deep.

The event concluded with Victoria Miss coming on stage and thanking everyone. Kannan stood there as everyone left, expecting someone to come to him too. But no one came. Kannan had the joy in his heart, about how well he did, but it was washed away by the waves of sadness which rose from the fact that there was no one to hug him.

"Hey Kannan. You were great on stage," Kannan heard a little voice call out to him

With a smile Kannan turned to see Ajai standing there, waiting for him. Both of them smiled at each other and walked with hands over the shoulders. The friends smile and appreciation made Kannan smile again. They walked through the school gates back home, both being there for the other.

There were many gathering where Amma made Kannan deliver the speech before uncles and friends, but Kannan felt the void every time he did. He had no one to lift him up in their arms and hug him. History was repeating itself with Narayan giving his first speech on Teachers' Day. But there was a difference this time, Kannan was there to see his son on stage and the eyes fill with a smile and take pride. He was there waiting to run up to him and hug him as soon as the speech finished.

41

Time tells the truth

Kannan was meeting Ramakrishnan Mama after a very long time, or rather should say he avoided meeting him just for that one incident.

"Hello Ramakrishnan Mama. How are you?" Kannan asked without a smile. His words were not from the heart. Even after 30 odd years, the scars of those words remain in his heart. Some moments are better avoided and forgotten than remembered and rekindle the emotions which hurt you.

Ramakrishnan Mama, Appa's cousin's husband, was a person who always had airs about him. Working for a private sector company, and the way he would talk would give a feeling as if he owned it. His salt and pepper well-combed hair, silver-rimmed glasses and dark complexion gave him a look, which Kannan was not so comfortable with. His smile did not have much of the warmth of love, or at least that's what Kannan thought. His son Sidhdharth Ramakrishnan was Kannan's playmate, the one of very few he had of his age or less, as Kannan was the youngest among the children in Appa's family.

"Kanna, how about going home and will be back in the evening?" asked Sidhdharth.

"Sure Sidhdhu. I will tell Amma and come soon," replied Kannan running towards home.

He went panting to the room where Amma was reading a magazine, one of her pastimes in the late afternoons. He reluctantly tugged Amma's saree.

"Amma, can I go to Sidhdhu's place and come back in the evening?"

Amma took her attention away from the article in which she was engrossed and did not even see Kannan coming in. Amma smiled and replied.

"Ok, be careful on the road."

"Amma, I am taking the cycle," Kannan had that wicked smile as it was his new found passion to roam around in his newly gifted BSA SLR.

Amma smiled and that smile said it all - permission granted.

Kannan ran to his BSA SLR, standing shining in deep red color with the rim and spokes shining in the afternoon sun. He mounted it with ease and started off. To gain speed, he would stand and pedal fast and rushed through the compound drive ways to reach the main road. It was as if he had conquered the road, when the shining cycle with the smiling Kannan on it sped through the roads. His soft hair would be flying back, eyes would shine, smile giving away the joy in his ride. Within no time he reached Sidhdhu's house which was just a few minutes away. The ten year old Kannan was tall enough to be mistaken for a teen. He looked around in pride and parked his cycle by the side. Locked it and took the key tossed it up in the air and caught it. He squeaked the metal gates and rang the bell. Sidhdhu opened the doors and looked at the shining cycle outside.

"Kanna, one ride," Siddhu pleadingly asked.

"No, Amma has asked me not to give the cycle to anyone," came the reply from the proud owner.

They went inside and Siddhu was so happy to have Kannan sound. Talks, games, music ... they had fun for over two hours when Ramakrishnan Mama reached home after work.

"So Kannan, new cycle?" asked Ramakrishnan Mama.

Kannan smiled and slowly got up. Kids always find it difficult to be themselves when elders are around. "It's getting late. I have to go now," said Kannan and waved at Siddhu and ran out of the house to his cycle and quickly vanished from sight with his speed.

A few days had gone by. It was a Saturday evening and as Kannan walked back home, he saw Ramakrishnan Mama standing there.

"Kanna, I would like to talk to you," said Ramakrishnan Mama.

Kannan went up to him and stood there silent. The regular sweet smile was missing as he did not know what Ramakrishnan Mama wanted from him. Did Siddhu complain about anything, or is it about the cycle? Thoughts hunted the ten year old.

"I want you to tell me the truth. You had come home last week and an audio cassette from my collection, the Jagjeet Singh Chitra Singh cassette, is missing. I want you to give it back.No one else has come home after that or before that."

Ramakrishnan Mama said in a stern voice with a smirk on his lips. He had kept his hand on Kannan's shoulder giving a feeling of being the investigating officer for a supremely important murder case was being solved there.

"ButI did not take it," said Kannan with the pain of being accused of something which he had not done.

"I am giving you time," said Ramakrishnan Mama.

Kannan's eyes turned red and tears started rolling down his fair cheeks. He pushed the hands from his shoulder and ran home. He threw himself to the bed and cried his heart out.

"I won't steal, I did not, I will never, but Ramakrishnan Mama believes I did so," Kannan was talking to himself. "Why would he say that? I did nothing wrong?" Kannan kept crying till the pillow was wet with the small boy's tears. He had not gone downstairs till late.

"Kanna," called Appa.

Kannan was shocked. Appa has come back from office. Did Ramakrishnan Mama complain about him? Is Appa calling to scold him? His thoughts ran wild. He slowly went down with his heart beating fast.

"My dear dearest Chandu, time for Dinner," Appa petted his beloved son and with one hand grabbed him with love. Kannan's heart came back to a normal tempo. There is nothing wrong, he thought. There was no talk about the cassette.

Days passed and it was almost a month since he had gone to Siddhu's house, far from normal. That evening while walking back home, he saw Ramakrishnan Mama talking to Mohan Periyappa, Kannan's paternal uncle. Kannan did not know whether to move forward or to retrace his steps. He walked towards home, with his ears awaiting a call and it was not long before he heard.

"Kanna."

It was Mohan Periyappa. Kannan did not look back but walked forward without a reply. He ran home and went straight to Amma. The wandering thoughts came back to

Kannan. Was Ramakrishnan Mama still hunting for his audio cassette? Why was he blamed for something he had never thought of?

"Mami," he heard Ramakrishnan Mama call Amma. "Where is Kannan?"

"He is here Ramakrishnan. Come inside. Tea?" Amma offered.

"No no, just had," he replied and walking in turned to Kannan. "You are not to be seen these days. Siddhu was asking about you."

Kannan remained silent.

"By the way, I got the cassette. I had given to my friend in the office. I forgot."

The moments of pain and anguish Kannan went through never let him smile with his full heart to Ramakrishnan Mama again. Blamed for nothing, making him a thief for a theft which never happened, the smirk on his face with the sense of accomplishment that he found the culprit, all made Kannan aloof from him. The friendship with Siddhu remained for a very long time, but the question still remains in Kannan's head. "Why was I blamed for something I did not do?"

Some words hurt you for a lifetime. As the thoughts got refreshed, Kannan took a pack from his bag and handed it over to Ramakrishnan Mama.

"The special collection of Jagjit Singh ghazals. This is an autographed special copy for you. I had got it for you in 2011 when he last came to Dubai. I had got it signed by him. He is no more now. So a rare piece for your collection." And Kannan smiled, smiled from the heart. The questions don't haunt him anymore.

42

Faces we see

"Is he the same person I know?" was the thought that lingered in Kannan's mind.

"How are you? Hope everything is fine with you? I met your Amma few months back and I was asking about you to her." Murugan Pillai's questions with a smile was the reason for Kannan to get lost in thoughts.

Kannan had met Murugan Pillai when he had to get his college forms attested by a gazetted officer. Priya, Kannan's classmate took him to her father for the same. A typical government servant whose life starts in the morning with work and ends with family and nothing else. He was dark-skinned, his well-oiled hair set to a style reminding of those who saw it villains of Tamil movies of the '70s. He wore brown shell framed glasses, old fashioned full sleeve shirt and trousers and his smile was a perfect dental ad one. Stern orthodox and a true believer in God, Murugan Pillai was a strict yet loving father. That image remained with Kannan till he fell in love with Priya and the college affair ended up in an adventurous marriage.

The smile and the question "Kannan, so how are you?How are studies progressing?" was only during the college days. After marriage Murugan Pillai's behavior toward Kannan was totally different. He was a doting father to his daughter and a proud father in law. The discussions they had were varied, from faith to politics, computers to office matters.

Kannan was reminded of yet another face of Murugan Pillai during the days when Kannan and Priya were staying with Appa and Amma after marriage. Kannan was back from work for the day.

"And she eloped with the guy next door. Velu knows this." That were the words from Murugan Pillai, who was at home when he walked in. He was talking to Appa in a very serious tone. Kannan smiled at them and walked in from a hectic day at work.

"And what happened to Kaveri?" Appa asked.

"Oh you did not know? She is suffering from cancer. Very critical," said Murugan Pillai.

Kannan saw a different Murugan Pillai, who was always hyper with work and home accounts, and Appa was listening to him eagerly. The others were inside the house discussing the new variety of sarees in the market and the ornament patterns that would have looked nice. Typical woman folk talk, nothing chauvinistic about it, but a fact of life.

Seeing everyone busy, Kannan went to his room, changed and got into comfortable home clothes. He could still hear about the fight of Kaveri and her husband, the problems in her workplace, her medical conditions and so on, the discussionbetween Appa and Murugan Pillai.

"Do I know her?" Kannan thought for a moment.

He went to the kitchen and got himself a cup of coffee. Sipping the hot cup of filter coffee, Kannan was trying to place the relation or the common factors which Appa and Murugan Pillai were talking about. As he was walking out of the kitchen, he saw Amma, Priya and Saraswathy, Priya's mother, his M-I-L, as they call it in the new lingo for mother-in-law chatting away to glory.

"Do you need anything?" asked Amma.

That question could have been avoided Kannan thought in his mind as he saw his MIL looking at Priya and Priya looking at Amma for a brief moment. No wife likes her MIL to take care of her son, as it is a constant struggle to prove who is better - wife or mother. Probably the fight between women were mainly based on that one point.

"No, no. I am fine. Carry on," said Kannan and walked to the front room where Appa and Murugan Pillai were still discussing at length.

"And you know the guy who drives that pink Maruti?" asked Murugan Pillai.

"Yes," said Appa.

Kannan was still not able to figure out what was going on and did not want to disturb the serious discussion between them.

"Pink Car! Totally impossible. Who would be driving a pink car of all the colors in the whole wide world," thought Kannan for a second and came back to the discussion. He saw Appa really paying attention. The matter would be really grave, otherwise Appa would not be listening so carefully, Kannan reached a conclusion in his mind and gave his attention too to the discussion. Murugan Pillai was seriously on it.

"He met with an accident. He is in the same hospital where Kaveri went for her check up yesterday. She did not see him, but he saw her…"

Appa's eyes were set in a gaze at Murugan Pillai who continued.

"She will need a surgery, but cannot afford it."

Is it some charity issue, Kannan thought, but kept it to himself as he did not want to disturb.

"Krishna will not be able to help?" Appa asked.

Now who on the Supreme Lord is this Krishna, Kannan was bewildered, and getting more irritated on not able to place these people in the mental list of family and friends. He sipped the coffee which was cold, when compared to the heat of the discussion.

"Krishna won't. He gave the money he had to his lover last week," replied Murugan Pillai.

It was getting too much for Kannan to digest and he interrupted.

"Who is Kaveri, who is Krishna and what is the discussion all about?" he broke his long kept silence.

All he could hear was laughter. Amma, Priya, MIL and FIL were laughing and Appa was laughing so much that Kannan saw Appa's eyes closed in the laugh.

"What happened? What's so funny about someone having cancer, not having money for treatment and accidents?" Kannan asked to clear the doubts that had started eating him.

"They are to catch up with what both of missed the previous week on their favorite serial on Sun TV, the 9'o'clock serial *Chiththi*," said Priya trying to control her laughter. Kannan also joined them in a rare happy moment.

Sharadha, Shakthi, Ramachandran, Vaidhegi, Prabhavathi, Krishna, Velumani, Kaveri, Vishwanathan,

Yogi, Viji, Anand, Prasad, Marudhappan, Charulatha, Daniel were more names which Kannan got used to in the next two years as he heard Appa and Murugan Pillai discuss whenever they met. 467 episodes running over nearly two years, got many glued to it and Kannan thought only ladies get addicted to serials, and thanked God for not being one of them.

It all ended when Priya left Kannan, owing to the looming difference of opinion between them. Four years of friendship in college, four years of courtship in marriage came to an end. It took four more years before the matter was to end with a petition for mutual consent for divorce in court. Kannan was on leave from his work in Dubai and came to the court for the final settlement, when the amount to be paid would be decided and all the emotions and memories would be legally erased from the minds of the couple. They would not be partners in crime called life.

The office of the advocate who was handling the case was really busy on the Monday morning. Kannan and Appa reached the office at 9 as instructed. The junior advocate was giving a whole lot of instructions, which Kannan hardly heard. All the hustle and bustle around him distracted his thoughts about what would happen next. The sounds of the typewriters being banged incessantly with words of dispute and settlement, the Police walking to the court with the convicts in handcuffs, the vendors selling stamp papers which would decide the fate of the people whose names would go on it, the vehicles carrying the judges to the court, who would decide what needs to happen in people's lives hampered by legal tussle, all were not strong enough to grab Kannan's attention.

A few minutes later Kannan saw a familiar face on a blue Vespa scooter with its indicator showing that it was coming towards him. It was Murugan Pillai with Priya as the pillion rider. The faces had no smiles. Not the smile which he had when he first signed the college forms, not the proud smiles when he introduced Kannan as his son in law to his colleagues, not the smile when he sat with Appa to discuss the missed episodes of serials, it was a frown which told Kannan only one thing, "You are the reason for what my daughter is going through now ..."

No smiles were exchanged, but the expenses laid out and discussions on how much would be the settlement money that had to be paid to take the divorce forward. As said in the famous folklore Kannan said to himself, "This too shall pass."

It was almost 10 years after the divorce that Kannan unexpectedly met Murugan Pillai in front of the temple. His hair had gone silver, but still oiled and groomed, the smile was back in his face, age had given him the wrinkles, but they joined in unison to smile at Kannan as if he were a long lost friend. With a smile Kannan replied.

"I am fine. Thank you. How are you uncle?"

For a brief moment in time, Kannan saw the different faces in a man's face - a respected government servant, a doting father, a proud father in law, a happy relative, a distressed father and what is left of him after a decade. People react not to people but the situations they are in, another life's lesson Kannan learnt that moment.

43

Eyes of the society

Kannan was on vacation for a few days and visiting Appa and Amma for a few days at least was the most divine of them all. They would sit till late night and chat about all that happened in the past, people, events, fun, sad memories, all were shared during those days, though Appa would sleep off while the chat continued. These few days were also not so different.

After a late night chat, and a nap, Kannan woke up early to visit the nearby temple.

"Amma, I will be back soon, going to the temple."

The morning breeze, the smell of incense and burning oil lamps in the air, the sound of the leaves in the trees whispering good luck to all those who walk by, the birds at their best, sounds of the devotional songs played loud from the temple, the vendors selling pooja items calling out for people to buy all that they need for the offerings. The whole atmosphere was different from the rest of the mornings Kannan enjoys in Dubai. As he entered the temple he saw a familiar face. A woman in her mid forties with a smiling face. Taller than usual, fair complexioned, slim, in a pink churidar, with metal framed glasses walk out of the temple gates with a cute child, her son, dressed in white shirt and denim shorts and moving towards her two wheeler, a white Honda Activa.

"Is that ..." Kannan tried to recollect the face, the smile.

He removed his slippers near the pillar where there was a guy sitting to take care of them, as the mystery of the missing slippers was a common story in all temples. Kannan smiled at him and walked the stone steps through the temple gates. he had gone just a few steps and he remembered.

"Vijayakka. Vasundhara Mami's daughter ... Akka's college mate... their old neighbor in Vasant Nagar."

Kannan was just in school when Akka and Vijayakka were in college together. They were good friends as being neighbors, they used to be together when they went to college or returned.

"She looks just the same, just a few grey hairs may be. For all that they had to go through," Kannan thought.

Flashes of memories took him back to those days. Vasundhara Mami and Krishnan Mama were staying opposite to their house and Vijayakka was their only daughter. They say it was a love marriage, but from the outside it seemed only marriage as the love had been washed out by liquor. Krishnan Mama who was an officer in a bank came every evening only drunk, not even knowing how to get out of the auto rickshaw he travelled in or to open the gates to enter the house.

"Appa," the helpless voice of Vijayakka could be heard almost every day by 8pm, when he used to come home drunk, not in senses. Vasundhara Mami would be holding on to the grilled gates of the house, with eyes wet with tears, seeing his plight. The two ladies would then drag him into the house with great difficulty. The next morning would greet Krishnan Mama at his best, well dressed prim and proper as if yesterday was just a dream.

That evening, it was the regular load shedding and the colony was lit with only candles and kerosene hurricane lamps or emergency light in some houses. The sound of the auto rickshaw stopping in front of Vijayakka's house could be heard. Vijayakka was standing outside waiting for her dad. But there was silence and Kannan saw Vasundhara Mami run to the auto rickshaw locking the grill with a lock. The auto sped across the colony roads in no time.

Vijayakka would never have to helplessly drag her Appa anymore. The ordeal was over or was yet to begin for the two women.

"Krishnan, Vijaya's father...he passed away," Kannan heard Amma tell Appa in the morning as he was getting ready to go to office.

On his way to the school, Kannan saw people gathering and heard cries from that house. He saw Amma too go inside Vijayakka's house as he reached the end of the colony road.

A week or two passed when everything was back to normal again. Vasundhara Mami would wear her helmet and whiz away to office, but without the usual smile on her face and Vijayakka continued her studies and would go with Akka to college.

One evening when Kannan was returning home from his evening playtime, he saw Swaminathan Mama talking to Amma, pointing fingers at Vijayakka's house.

"You know that woman is not good, she is having an affair with the contractor who was rebuilding the house. The news is out in her office too," Swami Mama told Amma.

Amma was silent. The news had spread like wild fire and the colony had hushed whispers about the affair. A kind man who wanted to help the two women in distress gets a bad name. Thanks to the society. Vasundhara Mami and Vijayakka remained home for weeks after work and study. Life was being made difficult for them by gossip mongers.

That was the time when a Mama and Mami had shifted to the upstairs' portion of Vijayakka's house. They were very pious. Mami was seen only wearing the 9 yard traditional Brahmin saree and Mama would be doing his Suryavandanam from the balcony. Everyone saw the tall fair good looking Mami with the brass pot full of water watering the Tulsi pot in the balcony, every morning. People had great regards for this devout couple. Kannan even heard the watchman telling the milkman.

"Sad that pious couple has to live in that characterless woman's house."

A month or two passed. A Police vehicle, an old blue Willy's with the typical black soft top, stopped in front of Vijayakka's house. The people around started peeping through the windows to know how Vasundhara Mami would be arrested and for what reason. The inspector stepped out from the front of the vehicle. Two constables stepped out of the back of the vehicle. Watchman was seen running to the venue of mystery. The constables opened the gates and stepped in. Kannan saw the fear in Vijayakka's face and a tear in Vasundhara Mami's face.

But for the surprise of everyone, they went upstairs, and what was left to see was the sight of the so called "traditional" Mama and Mami coming down the stairs with handcuffs on.

"For immoral traffic on a large scale," said many who enjoyed gossips.

That remained the talk of the colony for weeks. Kannan never understood what people meant by "large scale", but yes, the cat was out of the bag.

"Go quick. The darshan would be over in a few minutes for now," Kannan was brought back to the present by the temple staff, whom he knew well, but not his name. After coming back Kannan kept pondering over just one thing.

"Why does the society have a say on everyone's life?".

Vasundhara Mami had to face the brunt of the ruthless tongue of the society and so was Vijayakka taunted with vile comments by many. Kannan came to know from Amma that Vasundhara Mami passed away a few months back, and after that Vijayakka and her husband shifted to a house close by. Life has a lot in store and some said and some unsaid. But society has a say on anyone and everyone. Strange but true.

44

The night that was ...

"I don't want even to see your face." And the door closed on his face.

Those words from Priya were too harsh for him to take and Kannan was heartbroken. Silly household fights flare up when the fumes are given air by the words of those who should put it off. Misunderstandings, miscalculations and misinterpretations are all spinsters with a miss as a prefix, and with those in mind, we miss to live our life. Kannan got on his Enfield Bullet 350 and paused before he kicked it to life.

"Should I go home to Appa and Amma? They don't deserve to be hurt with our silly fights," Kannan thought as he changed the gear and the bike moved away. He broke his ride and looked back whether Priya is there at the window. But she was not. The night time roads were as lonely as his heart. With a heavy heart he rode away from her house. As the street lights, some lit and some flickering moved past his as he moved forward his thoughts were running faster.

"Enough… enough of this life" he thought to himself.

It was the same window which flashed in his mind. That night on Priya's birthday, when he had reached at the wee hours of night just to wish her a happy birthday, climbing the wall. He stood there then, watching her sleep in peace. Did not wake her but stood there looking at her. The same window where they used to stand together and wave at friends after the dinner gatherings. His heart was sinking like a rock in the sea and it hit the dumps of the bed.

In the meanwhile at home Amma was getting worried.

"Kannan is not yet home. It's getting late. Should I call Priya to find out?" Amma asked Appa. But he was silent.

Appa kept looking at the door and was waiting to hear the calling bell eagerly. He was a person who would be in bed at 10 but it was almost midnight and still no sign of Kannan. He went to his room, took an address book and was searching for some number. He frantically kept looking page after page and finally got it.

"I will call Ram. He would know or Kannan might be with him," Appa told Amma.

With eageryet sad eyes, Appa looked at the clock as he waited for Ram to pick the call.

"Good evening uncle," came the reply from Ram.

"Is Kannan with you? He has not called and is not yet home," Appa said to Ram.

"I will check," said Ram and hung up.

Kannan drove up to a lodge near the railway station. Central Lodge - he saw the board in front. The yellow board with faded red letters with a bulb that was more a veteran still serving the last few days in service. The dull light reflected his mood. The darkness around was his attitude towards his life. He entered the dim lit reception and saw a man sit on the chair behind it sleep.

"Excuse me," called Kannan with a shiver in his voice.

The man jolted awake as if he was attacked by a ghost.

"I need a room for one night," said Kannan.

Half in sleep, the man pushed the register in front of him and Kannan filled it up as if he was in a hurry. Yes. He was in a hurry to put an end to everything. The solution he had in his mind, was the decision many had taken at such junctures, to end his life. A shabbily dressed young boy led him to the room. He put his office bag on the wooden cot with dirty sheets and rock like pillow on one side of it. The smell of the laundry and the insecticide filled the room. The Lodge and the room seemed to be haunted or at least past living conditions, but still in use. Kannan was not in a mood to scrutinize the cleanliness or the condition of the room. All he had in mind was his last supper. He rang the once bright and yellow switch now darkened with dirt with a bell marked on it.

A few minutes later the young boy was at the door. "Sir, what do you want?" he asked.

"Something to eat. Vegetarian preferably," said Kannan.

"Dosa and rasa vada?" he asked.

Kannan took the money from his shirt pocket and gave it to the boy. As Kannan sat thinking about the mistakes and worries, which kept worrying him, the boy returned with a small red polythene bag with dosa and vada from the street vendors, wrapped in a newspaper. Kannan took the bag and the balance from the boy and was about to walk in to the room, when he stopped and turned to the boy who was still waiting there. He gave a 5 rupee note to him and smiled. A smile after hours of stress. The boy smiled back and took the money and ran happily through the dimly lit corridors of the lodge. The old clock on the walls of the corridor ticked loudly reminding Kannan of the little time left in his life.

At home, Amma was getting more restless and was pestering Appa with questions for which he had no answer. His tired eyes were red with sleep but couldn't get a wink of sleep. What was keeping Kannan so late and no calls from him yet, thought Appa.

The phone rang.

Amma picked the call and was silent. Appa could hear Priya shouting on the top of her voice on the other side of the call. Amma was not saying anything, but tears rolled down her eyes. The shouting continued for a while.

"I will talk to Kannan, everything will be alright," said Amma and kept the phone down. Appa and Amma exchanged glances and that said it all. Appa called Ram and informed him about the fight that was keeping Kannan away from home.

"Did he call you?" asked Appa.

"No. But don't worry. I will find him," said Ram.

Every moment of that night was taking long to move. The stillness of the night was just the opposite of the waves that lashed the old parents hearts.

Kannan quickly finished the dosa even without knowing how it tasted. At that moment it tasted like saw dust pancakes sloshed with water. He left the newspaper and the polythene cover on the table and washed his hands in the wash basin on the corner which was attacked by rust and dirt alike.

Kannan moved the left overs to a side and started writing on the writing pad he had in his office bag.

> *Dear all,*
>   *I say farewell to you all. Good bye. Have nothing more left in life. And I have nothing more to say.*
> *Kannan.*

The page was as blank as his mind then. He folded the letter and was writing the address on it, intending to leave it with the reception. That was when the mobile rang. Kannan was eager to see whether it was a call from Priya, but no. It was his friend Ram. Kannan left the mobile ringing, removing the ring he wore in his fingers and the chain from his neck with the

locket 'K' and put it in the office bag. He removed the watch and looked at the time for one last time. The phone rang again. It was Ram.

"Hello," Kannan answered with all the reluctance he had then.

"Da, I want to meet you now. The project you had designed has been approved. I want to meet you now," Ram was excited and went on talking with no response from Kannan. After a while he stopped and asked.

"Da. Are you okay? Where are you? I will come."

"Ok. I am in Central Lodge room 103."

Ram hung up with a quizzical feeling.

As time ticked forward, Kannan had made it up in his head that Ram would be the last person he would meet. Ram was trying to race against time, to reach out to Kannan and bring him back from the worried moments. Kannan was restless, thinking about all the happy and sad moments in life. He thought about his time with Appa, Amma, Thatha, Ammamma, Akka, Venki Mama, his school, college, the love, the passion, his art, and what not. Everything seemed to whiz past before his very own eyes. He heard a bike stop outside, breaking the silence and the sound of the crickets.

Kannan heard the knock and opened the door. It was Ram, smiling at his best. The tall, well built Ram with green eyes, was smiling like a child. His shirt was soiled but spirits high. His thick moustache gave him a beary feel, but he was breathing like a rabbit.

"Come. It's time to party," Ram dragged him out of the room. "Take whatever you want or leave it."

He dragged Kannan out of the room, who was being literally pulled and put on the bike. The kick on the starter and the adrenalin rush of the engine was all over the place tearing the silence away. Ram kept on talking while riding at his best speed possible. He screeched the bike to a halt and Kannan realized something he was not thinking of. Ram had stopped the bike in front of his own house, Appa and Amma were waiting at the gate.

"I knew it," said Ram and smiled at Kannan.

Kannan just walked in without even looking at Appa or Amma. Went to his room and dumped himself on the bed. It was almost morning and all night Appa and Amma were trying to find where Kannan had gone and what had happened to him. Ram shook hands with Appa and mounted his bike.

"Bye Uncle. He will be fine. Let him get some good sleep. I will come in the morning."

The moment was averted, and life had much more happiness in store for Kannan, which he would have lost the previous night. Ram had gifted a life in those few moments. Time wiped the thoughts of the night, but the pain still remains in the hearts of three people - Appa, Amma and Kannan.

45

A savings account of memories

It was after a very long time that Kannan went back to homeand was trying to clear the cupboard.

"Clutter has to be cleared," thought Kannan.

Amma came with his morning cup of filter coffee; steaming hot with strong smell of the freshly brewed coffee. It was different from all the mugs of coffee at the stores as it also had mothers love in it. Amma smiled and said, "After so many years, your cupboard is going to get a new life, at last."

Kannan smiled back, took the cup from Amma and sipped the cup of love. It was a unique feeling when the hot coffee went down his throat, refreshing him. He continued taking out old book, papers, files and all that had been stacked for years. Some old photographs, faded negatives in the translucent covers, note books, texts and so much more. The dust from them made him cough a bit, but the feeling of going back in time seeing the writings, the books and the memories associated with it was worth every moment of it.

He got a blue plastic bound book among the loads of things. He wiped it with a cloth and opened it.

New Bank of India... Kannan Iyer.... SB Account ... 1453.

It was the first ever bank account he had. Every small amount of money he got, be it for Vishu or from Periyamma as a reward for his achievements in academics as a blessing, or the small amounts of money he took from Appa for cleaning the car or selling old paper. All that went into the account sparing a bit for his books from the book store Paico. He went through each line of it and the first deposit of 5000 rupees dated March 12, 1984. He remembered walking into the bank along with Amma and starting the first ever bank account in his life with the money he got for his upanayanam. Appa had asked Amma to go with him to start the account. Saving little by little started with that day in his life.

When he got the blue passbook from the accountant at the teller counter, which he could hardly reach, the nine year old Kannan had a smile worth a million in the Swiss bank.

"Appa, I will clean the car every week," said the young Kannan. "Two rupees for car and one rupee for the scooter," was his demand.

Appa patted on his back with a glowing smile and said, "Done."

The hard earned money was stored in a box he kept secretly inside his study table which had a green sticker on the inner wall which read, "Chant Hare Krishna and be happy."

Every time he opened the desk he would look at the sticker and chant and then look at his safely saved money, to be deposited in the bank.

Months went by and every month Kannan would go with Amma to the bank to deposit the small amounts counting it with care every time he did. He would walk into the huge bank premises as if he owned the world tightly holding the red velvet pouch which Ammamma had given him and give it to the teller along with his pass book.

Kannan stopped the cleaning for a while and was seeing every small entry in the passbook. The money he had saved as a child. He saw a withdrawal entry in it.

"1500.00"

Kannan smiled looking at that entry. That was the time when Videocon had launched the economical version of a walkman. It was 300, as Kannan saw it in the sunday supplement of *Indian Express*. The advertisement enticed him, and he decided to buy one for himself.

"Amma, when are you going to the bank?" Kannan asked Amma who was busy preparing biriyani for lunch.

"Tomorrow. Why what happened? Deposit?" asked Amma stirring the masala which gave the kitchen a unique smell of the spices.

"No, I want to buy something. Withdrawal," Kannan said with a proud smile.

"Ok," replied Amma.

The day went looking forward to the next morning when he would go to the bank to withdraw money. Kannan checked again at night before sleep,

"Amma, take me to the bank. Okay?"

Tired with the day's work, with sleepy eyes, Amma removed her spectacles and kept on the bedside table and smiled affirmatively.

Kannan woke up early, finished his bath, prayers and got dressed up, ready to go to the bank with Amma. Every now and then he would go and check whether Amma is getting ready. And the moment he saw Amma ready he rushed and put his shiny black shoes on which he had kept polished the previous evening. He was looking at his best when he held Amma's hands and walked with her to the bank which was just a block away.

The person who took the red pouch every time looked at Kannan walk in and extended his arms as if to take the red pouch. Kannan smiled at him and said.

"No, I want to withdraw money."

His eyes sparkled as he took the withdrawal slip and signed it and gave it to Amma for her signature as it was mandatory for the guardian's signature for minor accounts. He took the money in his hands as Amma watched him take it with the brightest of expressions she had seen. He carefully put all the notes in the brown wallet he had hid in his back pocket, the one which he got when they shopped for the previous festival from the cloth store. The wallet had the emblem of the store embossed on it and the address of the shop printed in white inside.

"Amma, I will come soon. Can I go shopping?" asked Kannan.

For a 10 year old, he was taller and the town was known to him with his frequent visits to the book shops nearby.

"Careful," Amma said, "Cross the road with care and come back soon."

Kannan walked with the money in his pocket and kept looking back where Amma was standing in front of the bank seeing her son walk with his head held high. There was a smile on her which Kannan never could forget.

Kannan walked into the electronics shop and asked the person behind the counter where there was a huge hoarding of the newly launched Videocon Walkman.

"I want a Walkman," said the 10 year old to the salesman.

The salesman looked with wonder. He showed the small black box which had the three buttons on top and a headset.

"Do you want to see how it works?" he asked.

"Yes, please," replied Kannan.

He inserted the cassette and played it for Kannan and put the headset on the young boy's head. Kannan head the song ring in his head and just fell in love with the experience. "Private sound system," he thought to himself.

"Pack it please," said Kannan and took the purse out and carefully counted three notes of hundred and gave it to the salesman.

"At the cash counter please," said the salesman still not able to believe his eyes, seeing the small boy doing his shopping with style.

Walking out of the store, Kannan looked at the world outside, the bright new world where he had done shopping for himself, with his own money he had saved. He started walking back and saw a cloth store and the mannequin adorned with a peacock blue churidar with black leaves design on it. It looked very attractive. Kannan walked into the store after checking again for his wallet.

It was evening and Kannan was sipping the coffee Amma had given him and Akka walked in after her embroidery class, she used to attend, as it was holidays for both of them. Kannan looked at her enter and quickly rushed to the study room where he had unpacked the walkman and came back to the dining table with his walkman. Put on the headset and kept glancing at Akka, and her reactions seeing him have a new walkman.

"Oh new Walkman?" asked Akka.

"Yes. Mine," said Kannan.

The tease did not go well, but Akka kept her calm and asked.

"Can I see it?"

"Sure," was Kannan's reply.

He handed the walkman and switched it on for her and as she was listening to the song, ran back to the room. He opened the cupboard and took the white plastic carry bag which had a package in it. Came back in style and looked at Akka who was enjoying the song.

"This is for you. From me.Happy birthday," said Kannan.

The surprise and the smile on her face was priceless. She opened the package and it was the flowy peacock blue churidar for her from her little brother. Even till date, Akka has that churidar that her little brother had given her. Old but kept safe as a priceless possession, and Kannan knows it too.

Kannan sat down to write his diary that night after cleaning the cupboard and giving it a new life as Amma said. He wrote, "Money saved remains as it is. But spent for loved ones gifts you memories to treasure worth a million times its value," and smiled, putting his pen down.

46

Fragrance of life

The air outside was dry, and Kannan felt as if he could breath no more of the dry air around him. He walked in the busy lawyer's office and sat on the row of chairs in the lobby. The glass window behind him, open to the sky, had the sun setting and with it seemed as if Kannan's hopes were setting too. The thoughts just came back to him again and again.

"Sorry. It was nice working with you," the oversized HR Manager with his oddly placed spectacles on the tip of the nose said with a straight face devoid of any emotions, handing Kannan the relieving orders.

"But, you said," tried Kannan to reply but words were not coming to him.

He took the envelope and opened it. It had his tickets back home and the final cheque as the settlement amount. It was Kannan's efforts to save his colleague's job that held him responsible and had to take the brunt.

As he waited for his turn, Kannan was sitting with his heart sinking and eyes closed. It was then he had a strange feeling. A familiar fragrance, something which grabbed his attention. A tall man in white kurta, blue jacket over it and denims, in his fifties with salt and pepper well trimmed hair, walked with a bag in his hand dragged smoothly on the glassy floors of the office lobby stopped near him and turned and looked at Kannan.

"May I?" he asked with a smile which had a strange aura about it.

"Sure," said Kannan in a low voice.

"Murad," He extended his hands for a shake and Kannan reciprocated with a worried look in his face.

There were moments of silence, before Murad asked Kannan, "Would you like to have a coffee?"

Kannan smiled affirmatively, "Yes."

Murad walked to the coffee machine and took two cups from it. The whirring sound of the machine and the smell of coffeestarted relieving Kannan of the stress in his head.

"Do I really need to file a case to get the job back which I really don't need?" Kannan thought to himself, when Murad came back to the seat next to him and handed the cup of hot coffee. As they started sipping from the paper cup, Murad turned towards Kannan and said.

"You seemed to be too worried about something. Are you ok"

"Yeah. I lost my job yesterday and for no reason of mine," said Kannan.

"Oh that's sad. But how does it affect you?" asked Murad.

Kannan's brows knit in a strange expression as if asking why he would ever ask such a question.

"I mean, you are young and still have a great life ahead of you. Don't you see the positive in it?" asked Murad.

Kannan and Murad had a long chat regarding the misfortunes of life, the problems faced and the issues which sometimes grips a person strangling him to an emotionless stillness. And Murad said.

"My dear. Nothing comes before its time and nothing stays after its time."

His words were like instant magic potion which cleared the worries in Kannan's head.

"You can start fresh as long as you have the heart to do so," continued Murad. "If I were to brood at my problems at this age and you know no one comes to a lawyer's office for fun. I would not be smiling."

The air around him seemed to have a special fragrance - a fragrance which Kannan could not place where he felt the same before. Was it when he left Dubai in '98, was it when he got the call for a new job, was it when he received the award, was it when Narayan was born, was it when...? No, Kannan could not place it to any particular situation but was sure that the fragrance was very familiar.

"Thanks Murad Sir.Hope to see you again soon," said Kannan, and walked to the receptionist.

"Please cancel my appointment."

Kannan walked out of the lawyer's office and had a smile, a content smile on his face. Murad's face, the fragrance, the words all kept ringing in his head as he headed home, packed, went to the airport and reached back to Appa and Amma. As he entered 5 year old Narayan was smiling at him, dressed in a small white dhoti and a silky red shirt. Shining like a star, the smiles had something special.

"Ah, Kannan," Appa called out in surprise and excitement. "We were going to Guruvayoor. You never told that you would be coming," said Appa.

Amma was spell bound as she walked to the hall where Kannan was standing with his bags, straight from the airport.

"I will join you in a minute," said Kannan. He quickly washed and took a dhoti from Appa's cabinet and pulled a white shirt on. Tied his hair in a pony tail and brushed his salt and pepper beard quickly to shed the few drops of water in them after the wash.

"I will drive," said Kannanopening the passenger seat to Appa.

Appa smiled and got himself comfortable in the seat. Amma and Narayan sat in the back seat and the drive began with Hanuman chalisa playing on the stereo system with Kannan singing along. From time to time Kannan kept looking back as he drove and saw Narayan playing with his Ammamma and after a while tired and sleeping in her lap. The bhajans kept changing from one to the other and the drive seemed to lighten the worries in Kannan's head. He talked out the issues he had and his decision to start fresh again to Appa, who smiled and consoled him. By evening they reached the temple premises and Kannan parked the car and got out breathing the air around the place where millions come to shed their fears and a few tears.

Kannan held Narayan by his hand and the small boy kept looking at his Appa with a smile as Kannan looked at Appa with the same smile. Just the matter of age. As they reached the doors of the sanctum sanctorum, the people were calling out with faith.

"Krishna....   Guruvayoorappa....Bhaktavalsala.... Narayana ..."

And Narayan who had secured his place in his Appa's arms, hugged him and asked him in his ears. "Why are they calling me?"

Kannan smiled and gently patted on Narayan's face. He took the next step in and his eyes started flowing with tears. The same fragrance, the smell of sandal, flowers and tulsi ... the same fragrance, the one he experienced at every juncture of life when it changed... it was the same ... Kannan's eyes were overflowing with tears and the tears cleared the eyes for him to have a look at Guruvayoorappan himself, smiling.

With folded hands, faith in the heart, and Narayan by his side, Kannan knew one thing for sure looking at Guruvayoorappan. He comes in the form of many to lead him towards the right path. He just has to call him for help. After the darshan, Kannan's heart filled with joy as he received the prasadam from the poojari. The sandal paste, the few tulsi leaves and flowers in the leaf. Kannan put the sandal paste on Narayan's forehead and then on his own. He held the prasadam close to his face and took a deep breath.

"It's Him... It's Him..."

47

Everyday a celebration

Kannan was not sure whether it was late night or early morning, but he felt something touching him. A small soft hand on his face, on his beard, trying to pluck his beard. The hand smelt of baby lotion and powder, more it smelt of love. The soft skin on the palms were like feathers of silk. The curly long hair on the forehead were like overflowing honey from a jar of sweetness, or that's how Kannan felt when he saw it. He heard the giggles of love and his eyes saw his son trying to wake him up. Those giggles were more than any sweet music of the world to Kannan's ears. Narayan. The bright big eyes, sweet smiles, big nose and drool sweet lips calling out to him. He was the reason for Kannan's smiles day or night. He lifted him with both his hands and placed the small Narayan on his chest and asked.

"Are you not tired of playing with me? Now what does my Narayan want?"

"Gaaa... gurr...he..."

Hardly did Kannan understand anything but that was what Narayan told him sitting on his chest as if he had mounted the biggest tusker on the earth. His hands were still reaching out to his salt and pepper beard. Kannan moved his head and held him with one hand and reached out to the spectacles on the side table. The night lamp was switched on and the spread smelt of baby powder alone. The sun was rising in a while and the sky was slowly turning its shade. The mild orange light was peeping through the window and the glow on Narayan's face made him look divine. His curly hair and the smile made Kannan call out to him.

"Narayana ... Gopala... Kanna..."

And for every name called out the small Narayan nodded his head as if he understood everything. Kannan lifted him up as he got up, put him on the bed and started playing with him. Kannan with his warm hands rubbed Narayan belly and he would start laughing. He would softly hit the tummy with his head and he would laugh more. Kannan rubbed his nose on the stomach and the baby laughs would fill the room, slowly getting lit by the sun, who was smiling outside seeing the father and son play early in the morning.

Kannan lifted Narayan and placed him close to his heart in a warm hug and walked towards the kitchen. Kannan boiled the milk while singing and adoring the little Narayan.

Krishna Krishna Mukunda Janardana ... Krishna Govinda... Narayana..., he would pause and sing again *Narayana...* as the little Narayan would look surprised at his Appa singing songs for him. His eyes would sparkle as Kannan called out "Narayana" in between. The sparkle said it all. Kannan would smile as soon as he sees the sparkle in the big eyes. Every blink of the eye was magnetic and so captive. Kannan softly kissed the soft ball of wool cheeks and continued singing.

Krishna Krishna Mukunda Janardana ... Krishna Govinda... Narayana...

Narayan would giggle to the song as if he was trying to sing along with his Appa. Kannan carefully managed to hold Narayan in one arm and cool the hot milk carefully with the other. He poured the slightly warm milk in the bottle, sweetened it with sugar and poured a drop on to his skin to check the warmth and a drop on to his tongue to check the sweetness.

"Yes, it's warm and sweet," Kannan thought to himself.

"Come one come one my sweet one. Time for your morning milk," said Kannan as softly as he could. The whispers reached the sweet big ears of Narayan and he blinked in affirmation. The lips were still drooling and Kannan pulled out a soft napkin from the box and wiped Narayan's lips. Narayan would not stop looking at Kannan while he happily drank the sweet milk from the bottle. His hands were still on Kannan's beard and pulling them with all the strength those little hands had. The nipple of the bottle was trying to hide the smiles of Narayan as he did smile with every attempt of his to pull the beard out failed.

Kannan carefully put Narayan to bed and lay down next to him on his side. The warmth of Kannan's body brought Narayan more closer to him as he was slowly dozing off with smiles on his lips. Kannan kept gazing at the sleepy eyes as Narayan gently closed them. The eyes seem to slow down the world, gently with all the love in the world. To put him to a sleep... Kannan softy sang a lullaby that always put Narayan to sleep.

Omana thinkal kidavo ... nalla ... komala thaamara poovo...

Is it the lines of Irayimman Thampi for Swathi Thirunaal or the rag Neelaambari or the love Kannan had for Narayan was debatable. But the lines put Narayan to a sound sleep. Kannan unknowingly slept with Narayan alongside like a baby.

Kannan was woken up by a touch on his shoulder. Firm hands, warm and Kannan woke up from the sleep to see a tall man, fair skinned, with the same bright big eyes, long hair, sweet smile and the long nose.

"Happy birthday, Appa."

It was Narayan and old Kannan with long white beard and skin aged with wrinkles, still having the sweet smile as ever woke up to a morning hug from his 20 year old son. Kannan rubbed his eyes and looked at the most auspicious gift God had given him 20 years back - Narayan. The father and son exchanged hugs and Kannan said, in the deep old voice.

"Even my dreams are full of you. There was a time when my dreams were of the future. But now my memories have turned to be my dreams."

Narayan held Kannan's hand and the tall old man with the slight hunch of age took the shoulder of his young son, who looked exactly like the 20 year old Kannan. As they walked from the bedroom to the kitchen for their regular morning coffee, which Narayan made for Kannan.

"God sometimes gives you rare gifts and you are mine. Every day is a celebration with you," said Kannan.

And it was another birthday celebration at Kannan's home over a cup of coffee, the son made for his father.

48

The bedtime story

"Narayan," Kannan called out to his 16 year old sweetheart.

"Son, it's time for the bed time story," said Kannan.

"I'm coming Appa," said Narayan.

Kannan, at 56 was all excited and was restless like a five-year-old. Dinner was over and Kannan walked towards the garden outside the house and to wait for his son Narayan.

"I am here outside in the garden Narayana."

The nightfall had a special feeling in the hill station. Kannan had been living there, with Narayan, for more than a year now. The stars were shining so close to the mountain, Kannan felt he was in the paradise. It was a full moon night and the moonlight was like a spot light on the Garden. The white full plate on the sky with heavenly mead porridge in it, waiting to feed the hungry shining stars around it. Kannan breathed in fresh air with the smell of pine cones and eucalyptus all around.

"Appa .... Thatha used to tell you stories?" Narayan asked. The bright young eyes of Narayan were shining just like the stars when he asked the question. Tall, bright faced, with long hair like his Appa and in the loose white pyjama kurta, Narayan looked more angelic in the moonlight. Kannan laughed at Narayan's question and started looking at his son, who looked the same as when he was in his teens, if not better.

"Akka and I very well know that in Ramayana, Dasarath had four children and they were Ram, Lakshman, Bharath and Shatrughna. Thanks to your Gopal Thatha."

Kannan sat down on the white cast iron garden chair with soft cushions on it, in the green lawn lit by the moon. He sipped the cup of coffee Narayan gave him with a smile. It has been a hard to break habit for Kannan since childhood that he could sleep well only if he had coffee.

"Akka and I used to pester your Gopal Thatha to tell us stories," said Kannan thinking about his childhood days.

The house used to be doldrums of activities at night. Amma settling with her daily chores of washing after dinner, Appa patting the bed to make it for all, Kannan and Pachai working on their bags for the next day at school and everyone would be busy bees after dinner. Once the sheets were on, the blankets in place and the last dish washed all would be at the gateway to the dream world, the bedroom. Amma would be tired and would be the first to hit the bed. Appa would be joined by Pachai and Kannan with their regular requests.

"Appa story ... Appa story ...."

And Appa would start with a smile. Tired after a whole day's work in his eyes so red like an apple, he would make all the efforts to keep them open. Kannan would sit on his stomach and beat his chest to tell them a story. Each one of them would be in their respective positions, Amma on the left corner, then Kannan with his favorite black blanket, Appa next and then Pachai.

"In a far of land called Ayodhya, there was a king called Dasarath. He had four sons. Eldest was Ram, then Lakshman, then Bharat and then Shatrugna. They grew up together and their upanayanam (initiation) function was conducted…"

By the time he reached the portion of the four sons being initiated spiritually Appa would have initiated his dream trip to sleep. His eyes would close with the days fatigue and his big nose and mouth start with a light snore. As soon as he dozed off, from both sides the attack would start.

"Appa Appa … then what happened?" Kannan and Pachai together.

Appa would startle and wake up with a jolt and start all over again.

"There was a very nice king in Ayodhya, and he was called Dasarath. He had four sons. Eldest was Ram, then Lakshman, then Bharat and then Shatrugna. They grew up together and their upanayanam function was conducted …"

Again the sleep fairy would have put Appa to sleep again. The way the Ramayana start would differ, but the content remained the same. For a very long time Kannan and Pachai only knew the initial part of Ramayana as Appa had only one story to tell them. The sleep fairy would finally put everyone to rest, gifting each one with dreams of their choice. Amma would dream of buying a new refrigerator or a new house or about her brothers, Appa would be dreaming about the account statements or balance sheets or profit and loss accounts, Kannan would be dreaming about the school drama or the cousins and friends, and Pachai obviously would be having dreams about writing exams and studies alone.

"That's what we knew about Ramayana from your Gopal Thatha," concluded Kannan with a chuckle.

Narayan laughed a hearty one and said.

"Appa, it's too cold outside. I know you like cold, but it's no fun to fall sick in this mountain. Come, come inside. Bedtime story time."

They both walked in a hug and went to the warm and cozy bedroom. Kannan removed his home shoes and kept it in the rack, Narayan followed. As Kannan tucked Narayan to bed and got himself inside a warm quilt, Narayan took a book out switched the bed light on and switched off the main lights of the bedroom.

Kannan hugged Narayan in a warm hug and looked at his son eagerly, when he started.

"Once upon a time in a far off beach, it rained heavily and the sea got rough. The sea hit the land and lashed all its anger on him. The land smiled and held her in his arms. He said to her,

"I will be there for you always". The summer sun scorched the land and he was burning hot as if he had fever. The waves hit the sand gently and said, "Shhhhh ... everything will be all right", and washed away all his tears...."

By the time Narayan finished the line, Kannan was fast asleep in a hug. Since the time Narayan could read, every night was a bedtime story time and Narayan would read the very same story to his Appa to put him to sleep. Narayan smiled, carefully, without making any sounds folded the book written by his Appa for kids years back, switched the reading lamp off and tucked himself to the hug and slept, waiting for another day and another night, when he would read the story again find his Appa sleeping with a smilehugging him.

49

A special birthday

"Sir." Benson woke Kannan who had dozed off in the car. For the past one month, Kannan and Benson were on a spree to catch a glimpse of Kannan's life. Every day was filled with travel and sights and sounds. And every night ended in a room, cozy enough to get some sleep and more importantly get a space to jot down the memories in a file. Sheets of blank white paper turned to be the testimonials of an eventful life. Every memory had its own significance in Kannan's life. As Benson would snore away to sleep, Kannan would careful jot down all that had brushed through his mind that day.

"So, you take an off for a week. Take rest. Good night *sarathy,*" said Kannan as he walked with his file held close to his chest. Benson followed him with the bags and kept them in Kannan's room. Kannan slept peacefully that night, with dreams filled with smiles, waiting for the day break - the very special one.

The ripe old age never dimmed the shining eyes of the septuagenarian Kannan. The morning was very special for him. The day of transition from the seventies to eighties. The long grey hair fell on his wrinkled face like a wild waterfall. The cascading hair gave him the grace which partly covered the eyes that woke up to the special day with a glitter in it. Kannan slowly helped himself up forgetting the aching pain which had took a part of the sleep the night before. He had the smile which every birthday boy has in his childhood or the teens. He could hear some rattling of the spoons and plates in the kitchen.

"Happy birthday Appa."

Kannan heard the voice from the entrance where the tall man Narayan, in his late thirties was standing with a smile. Holding a surprise in his hands. Yes, the birthday cake with the sinful icing for Kannan's age. The flames of the candles seemed to dance to the tune of the birthday song his son was singing for him, as he held gracefully the small cake he had baked himself. It was a birthday special gift to his dad and the man who gave him the passion to bake.

The birthday was very special to Kannan and for Narayan. Two years into Narayan's marriage, the dear couple would be blessed with a bundle of joy any time now. It was Kannan's birthday and would be double the joy with the new member in the family. Narayan had a smile, the smile of a proud father, when a part of his life comes to the whole wide world.

Kannan walked up to his son and hugged him. He held the fresh smiling face in the wrinkled hands like a twiggy nest nestles the singing nightingale. The smile was so precious to Kannan that looking at it, he smiled his best.

"So today is the big day. I will be ready in ten minutes. I can't wait,"

Kannan blew the candles and they both happily helped themselves with the delicious piece of cake quickly. Narayan wiped his mouth with a tissue finishing the piece of cake and nodded his head in approval. As Kannan got ready, Narayan was picking up this and that and putting it in the bag to take to the hospital. The bags were ready, Kannan dressed himself in his typical white long kurta and pyjama and Narayan was looking his best in his baby pink shirt and blue jeans.

As they got into the car, Narayan clicked the seat belts safe and saw his dad clutch on to a file with a bundle of written sheets.

"Appa, what's this file? Do you really need them?"

"Yes," Kannan smiled as he adjusted his spectacles up closer to his eyes on the long nose.

"It's my gift for you? Will tell you. We have a long time ahead of us."

The sun was shining bright and smiling at all the sunflowers in the garden. The father and son smiled with excitement and anxiety. They reached the hospital parking area and got out of the car. As Narayan was picking up the bags from the car, Kannan slowly walked towards the entrance without saying anything. Narayan followed managing the bags clumsily.

The corridors of the hospital were buzzing with activity. As they reached the room, the nurse from the nurse's station came towards Narayan.

"Mr. Narayan, we just took your wife to the labour room. You can wait outside there or remain in the room."

"Can I?"

"Oh sure. You can go in if you want. Just get the scrubs in the room near the labour room."

The father and son exchanged smiling looks and Narayan kept the bags in the room and rushed to the room next to the labour room round the corner. Kannan walked up to the chairs outside the labour room and waited; waited for the moment, and the wait seemed to be endless for him. He remembered the wait similar to the one this day, when he was waiting for Narayan to come to him.

Kannan kept looking at his watch and chanting with his prayer beads from time to time. It was an hour later, that Kannan heard the most beautiful music to his ears - the cry of his grandchild from inside. Kannan started walking up and down the corridor impatiently with the smile he could not resist. His heart was blooming with happiness.

"It's the grace of God. Thank you, God," Kannan kept saying to himself till he heard the door squeak open.

Kannan turned around to see a blurry image of someone standing at the door in green. Kannan wiped his eyes of the tears that had blurred his sight and adjusted his spectacles to see the image that gave him the heavens. It was Narayan in green scrubs with a white bundle of happiness in his hands. As he walked towards Narayan, Kannan could it see the child more and more clear. He could see two pink lotuses out of the white cloth, the two sweet tender feet.

"It's your grandson Appa. He wants to see you. It's my birthday gift to you."

Kannan could not stop the tears flowing out in joy. He saw the pink face of his grandson; eyes closed peacefully, wrapped up comfortably in white, he was the prettiest flower he had ever seen. Kannan kept wiping away the tears and rubbed his hands in excitement. He gently touched the feet to see the tiny toes curl up. He was soft as the morning cloud. He wore a smile, the most enviable one.

Kannan opened the small Vishnusahasranamam book from his pocket and opened it. Ran his fingers through the lines and looked up to Narayan, who was standing there looking at his father and his son.

"Rishikesh Narayan," Kannan said with his voice shuddered with excitement.

Narayan closed his eyes in approval, still holding on to the future.

"Please take the child to the mother," said the nurse who walked out of the labour room.

Narayan walked in and Kannan walked to the chair where he was sitting. He had left the file of handwritten sheets of paper there on the seat. He went and picked the file and clutched it close to his chest as if the file was his child.

Narayan went to the room, changed the scrubs and walked towards his Appa. Kannan was still holding on to the file close to his chest with one hand and chanting on the prayer beards on the right hand.

"Appa," called out Narayan.

"God bless you," said Kannan opening his moist eyelids.

Kannan put the prayer beards in his Kurta pocket and extended the file towards Narayan. Narayan took the file and read the beautifully written cover which read:

All I Need Is a Hug

"It's a collection of my memories. That's all I have for you now for giving me the most precious gift," said Kannan.

Narayan hugged Kannan as the moment turned out to be the most beautiful moment Kannan had been waiting for.

"These are the sights and sounds of my life and there is more to tell you. Will tell you more, God willing," Kannan told Narayan in his ears as the father and son were lost in a hug. And as Kannan's friend had told him once

"All you need is a hug."

For all life had taught me …
Kriss Venugopal

CPSIA information can be obtained
at www.ICGtesting.com
Printed in the USA
BVHW071030080419
544914BV00012B/326/P